She shouldn't do this

Erin had sworn off men...although, at this moment with her palm against Jack's hard, warm chest, for the life of her she couldn't remember why. Moving her hands in small circles, she worked her way along his torso, her pulse thudding as she traced his firm muscles. Desire flowed through her and she swallowed as he rolled back his head and a small moan of pleasure sounded from his throat.

It wasn't enough. She had to touch him.

With quick twists of her fingers she undid his shirt, then laid her hands on his skin, hardly believing she could be so bold. Where was that resolve to remain single? Nowhere in sight.

His gaze fell to her mouth and she could feel him fighting the urge to kiss her. She struggled herself. In that moment there wasn't anything that made sense in the world but joining her mouth to his. She pressed her lips to his, where she paused for just a heartbeat while their breath mixed, the warmth and excitement and anticipation almost unbearable.

So much for swearing off men.

ROMANCE

Blaze™

Dear Reader,

As I was growing up, the children of my family split into two distinct groups—the big kids and the little kids. Falling directly in the middle of the seven of us, I could have gone either way. To my frustration, though, I was relegated to the latter group, always left out of the big kids' fun. As a result, I completely relate to the issues my heroine in *Faking It,* Erin McClellan, faces as a younger sister.

I hope you like my story of how Erin struggles to gain acceptance and carve her own place in her family. I enjoyed matching her with Jack Langston, a hero I wouldn't mind meeting in real life.

If you get a chance, write me and let me know what you thought of this story and the SEXUAL HEALING miniseries. I value my reader feedback. You can reach me at dorie@doriegraham.com or P.O. Box 769012, Roswell, Georgia 30076. And don't forget to check out my Web site at www.doriegraham.com.

Best wishes,

Dorie Graham

Books by Dorie Graham

HARLEQUIN BLAZE

39—THE LAST VIRGIN
58—TEMPTING ADAM
130—EYE CANDY
196—THE MORNING AFTER *
202—SO MANY MEN…*

*Sexual Healing

FAKING IT
Dorie Graham

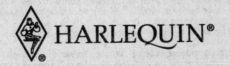

TORONTO • NEW YORK • LONDON
AMSTERDAM • PARIS • SYDNEY • HAMBURG
STOCKHOLM • ATHENS • TOKYO • MILAN • MADRID
PRAGUE • WARSAW • BUDAPEST • AUCKLAND

Rain, Newt and Lily, you are by far the most influential group of sisters to have touched my life. You challenge me in ways that help me grow, fill me with pride in all your accomplishments and bring me more joy than I could ever have imagined.
I love you for always. This one's for you.

ISBN 0-373-79212-3

FAKING IT

Copyright © 2005 by Dorene Graham.

This edition published by arrangement with Harlequin Books S.A.

® and TM are trademarks of the publisher. Trademarks indicated with ® are registered in the United States Patent and Trademark Office, the Canadian Trade Marks Office and in other countries.

www.eHarlequin.com

Printed in U.S.A.

1

SHE WAS TYPHOID MARY reincarnated. Erin McClellan stared in horror as Trent Gray heaved the contents of his stomach into the vase she'd shoved into his hands just in the nick of time. The flowers that had occupied the vase lay limply beside a discarded condom wrapper. Guilt swamped her. She stared at the wrapper as Trent bent again over the vase, clutching his stomach.

If only she could blot out the sounds of his agony as he heaved again. She could kick herself for letting this happen. Hadn't she learned with Ryan, the last man she'd slept with?

Trent raised his head and she took the vase and set it aside as he flopped weakly onto the pillow. How could she have done this to such a nice man?

If only her sister's friend, Josh, hadn't introduced them and Trent hadn't been willing to take over for Josh, who'd been helping her with her design projects. If only she and Trent hadn't spent all that time together. If only Trent hadn't talked with her late into the night about all her dreams and her worries, making her feel first safe, then vulnerable in a way that had her melting into his arms. If only his lips hadn't been so soft, his kisses so hot.

If only she hadn't given in to temptation and slept with the man.

"I'm so sorry." She mopped his forehead with a cool cloth.

He raised his bleary eyes to her. "Don't worry. It isn't your fault."

If only he knew.

"Well, I feel responsible." She held the vase away from her. "I'll get you a drink of water."

He nodded. She left him to pad down the hall to her kitchen. She left the vase to soak in the sink, then poured him a glass of water.

As she walked slowly to her room, her mind drifted over her past relationships. That first time with that guy from the park that neither of her sisters, Tess or Nikki, knew about had been surprising at best. She'd been concerned when he'd become ill after they first made love but had chalked it up to bad timing.

The second time he'd gotten ill after their love-making, she'd thought he'd just needed more time to recuperate. When it happened again after some time had passed, she'd placed the blame squarely on his shoulders, thinking it was some strange quirk on his part. How shocked she'd been when he'd broken up with her, saying he couldn't take it anymore.

Then she'd met Pete and the same thing had happened again. She'd somehow talked herself into believing it was all some weird coincidence. Surely none of this was *her* fault.

Pete had come and gone rather quickly and she'd begun to think it was all an unpleasant dream. Then she'd met Ryan, and after four days of him being too sick for her to sneak him out of her bedroom, she'd known.

It *was* her.

"Here." She handed Trent the water.

He took a feeble sip, then shook his head. "This is so embarrassing. I swear, I never get sick."

"Don't worry about it." She looked anywhere but at him.

He wrestled himself into a sitting position. "I should probably go."

"Can you drive?" She cringed at the note of hope in her voice.

"I think so. I'm sorry about this, Erin."

"You have no need to apologize." She helped him dress, shamefully grateful to have him leaving. If she had to go through another catastrophe as she'd gone through with Ryan, she might just jump out the window.

"Are you sure you'll be okay?" Guilt returned to weigh her down as she walked Trent to the door. "I can drive you…or you could stay."

His eyes widened. "No, it isn't that far." He gripped the doorjamb. "I can make it. I'll recuperate faster in my own bed."

"Right. I'm sorry again about…" She gestured lamely, feeling three times an idiot and hating herself for causing him such discomfort.

After nodding awkwardly, he lurched out the door. Relieved beyond measure, she turned the dead bolt behind him. At least her sisters had moved out. The thought of discussing her little problem with them sent dread twisting through her. They'd never taken her seriously. Why would this be different?

She'd avoided an interrogation over Ryan only by refusing to discuss the issue, and they'd taken her silence for heartache. In this case, they might not have given up so easily. The last thing she felt like doing was explaining what had happened with this latest love interest.

Where both of you inherited the wonderful gift of sexual healing, I seem to be experiencing some kind of quirk in the gene pool. You sleep with a guy and he comes out of it revived and ready to conquer the world. I sleep with a guy and he ends up so ill he wishes he could die.

She let her gaze sweep the apartment that had been home to her and her sisters for the past several years. Memories flooded her: bumping into one of Nikki's lovers as he made a hasty but ecstatic exit in the middle of the night. Tess's ex-lovers falling all over themselves to please her sister and never taking notice of Erin; the old guy next door leering at her after a particularly high-traffic day.

It was time for a change. Her lease was nearly up and she didn't need such a big place all to herself. Nikki and Tess had moved on with their prospective lives—they had both issued invitations for her to move in, but the thought of living with either of them sent unease racing through her. Besides that, they were both basking in glorious love affairs and the two had embraced Aunt Sophie's ridiculous assertion that the three of them had descended from a long line of sexual healers.

"Sexual healers." Erin's mouth quirked into a lopsided grin.

"Sexual healers." A giggle tickled its way up her throat.

"Sexual healers." Laughter burst from her in a rush of nerves and incredulity.

She laughed until she sank to the floor, her back to the wall. She pressed the heels of her hands to her eyes. How could they have bought in to such foolishness?

Hurt and resentment swirled through her. When they had been kids, she'd been excluded from all the fun, and as they'd grown up, she'd been left out of all the more serious discussions. Things had improved and she'd come to terms with being the youngest sister, but her sisters' acceptance of this "gift" felt too much like a betrayal. Logically she knew it wasn't, but the feeling had lodged itself in her and she hadn't been able to shake it.

Again she let her gaze sweep the empty rooms that had once overflowed with Nikki, Tess and Tess's minions, as they called her collection of men. The quiet settled around Erin and she breathed deeply, savoring the peace. She'd had so little peace sharing this apartment with them. She had no desire to stay in a place tainted by less-than-happy memories.

It was time to move. She longed for something different, a *normal* place, where no one talked about empathic natures, Aunt Sophie's brews or sexual healing—a place far removed from the McClellan lore.

"WHY IS THIS ESTIMATE SO HIGH?" Jack Langston frowned over the total on the work order from the electrician his mother had contracted.

"These fixtures aren't up to code. They need fireboxes installed. When was this house built?" the electrician asked.

"Sometime in the seventies?" Jack glanced at his mother for confirmation. He'd grown up in this house and they'd always had the same lighting fixtures.

His mother shrugged. "Seventy-four, I think. These are probably the original fixtures."

"Yes, ma'am, you were lucky when this shorted it didn't start a fire," the electrician said. "I can't install the new lights without first putting in fireboxes."

"Jack, when you're done with that, do you have a minute?" His mother's sister, Rose, peered over the electrician's shoulder. "I can't decide about this new insurance policy. I've been putting this off forever and my current policy is about to expire. I need to make a decision today. I could use your advice."

Jack's cell phone buzzed in his pocket. "Hold on a minute, Aunt Rose." Rubbing the tightening in his chest he answered his phone. "Jack Langston."

"Hey, bro, what's up?" his brother, Bobby, asked in his usual laid back manner.

"Trying to help out Mom and Aunt Rose." The heaviness in Jack's chest increased as he glanced at his watch. If he didn't tie things up soon, he'd be late for his one o'clock appointment with a new client.

"Great, you're at Mom's?" Bobby asked. "I'm right around the corner dropping off my car. Do you think you can swing by and get me, then take me back to my place?"

The heaviness grew into a dull ache as Jack's gaze drifted over the electrician, his aunt and his mother, with her worried frown. His cardiologist's words rang in his ears.

You've got to cut back, not push yourself so hard. This fatigue and these chest pains are your body's way of warning you that all isn't as it should be.

But Jack was fine and how could he let his family down? "Give me about fifteen minutes to finish up here, Bobby, then I'll come get you."

His brother gave him directions to the garage, then Jack hung up and turned to the electrician, saying, "Go ahead and replace both fixtures and install the new fireboxes."

"But, Jack," his mother said, "I'm not sure I can afford that right now." She turned to the electrician. "Maybe you should come back at the end of the month?"

"He's here, Mom, let him do the work. I'll take care of it." Jack gave her arm a reassuring squeeze.

"Sweetheart, are you sure? I hate to count on you all the time like this."

"Not to worry. I'm here to look after you." He spent a few more minutes with the electrician, before he felt satisfied the man would do the job to his specifications, then he turned to his aunt. "Okay, Aunt Rose, I have exactly one minute. How can I help?"

Fifteen minutes later he raced for his car. His aunt had had questions about everything from deductibles to flood insurance, with a sidetrack on term life insurance. In the end, she'd opted to renew her current policy.

He shifted, trying to ease the tightness in his chest as he sat at a light on his way to pick up Bobby. Why had he told his brother he would get him? Jack would have to hurry and make every light on his way to meet his client.

The light turned green and Jack sped on. Ten minutes later he pulled up in front of the garage where Bobby said he'd be, but his brother was nowhere in sight. Jack slammed his door shut, then hurried into the low brick building. A kid with a Mohawk greeted him at the counter.

"I'm looking for my brother. He just dropped his car off here."

"Yeah, looks kind of like you. He ran across the street. Said he'd be right back."

"Across the street?" Jack turned to look where the kid pointed. An adult novelty shop. Jack's frustration burned into anger. "Thanks."

He hurried across the street, running to avoid an approaching sixteen wheeler. Bobby's platinum head was clearly visible through the wide front window of the shop. Jack entered to find his brother leaning

over the counter flirting with the young woman behind it.

He turned as Jack entered. "Hey, big brother, this
is Deloris. She says they're having a sale on whips.
You want one?"

"It's time to go, Bobby. I have to make it to a
meeting by one."

Bobby groaned. "Sorry, Deloris, got to go. Maybe
I could call you some time?"

"Bobby," Jack said, putting the tone of authority
into his voice that their father had used all those years
ago and that Jack had perfected when he'd stepped
in to fill his father's shoes.

"A guy can't have any fun around here anymore."
Bobby cast Deloris one more look filled with longing,
then followed Jack to the door. "Your timing sucks."

"You're welcome," Jack said as he slid into the car.

"Okay, thanks for giving me a ride." Bobby
grinned, oblivious to all but the pretty brunette as he
craned his neck to catch one last glimpse.

"You can pick up where you left off when you
come back to get your car," Jack said.

"If she happens to be working then."

"I have never known you to have trouble getting
a date."

"True." Bobby cranked up the radio as Jack drove
to his brother's apartment.

A short while later Jack dropped off Bobby, then sped toward the interstate, his pulse pounding through the dull ache in his chest. The light ahead turned yellow. Jack floored it, rubbing his chest in an effort to relieve the growing pressure there.

The radio disc jockey announced the time and Jack swore. He was going to be late, even if he hit all green lights. He should call his client. Steering with one hand, he reached into his briefcase for the file with the client's contact information. The file spilled as he yanked it from the briefcase, scattering its contents over the front seat and floor.

The ache radiated from his chest, with a sharpness that took his breath. Grimacing, he pressed his hand to his heart as the pain escalated to agonizing proportions.

A horn honked. He glanced up, then jerked the wheel hard to the right to avoid an oncoming car. The road veered off to the left as the car careened over the shoulder. He braked hard, fighting to maintain control of the wheel. All the while, he clutched his chest and gasped for breath through the bone-numbing pain.

His car hit an embankment and stopped. Adrenaline pounded through Jack as he peered at the back of the other car as it continued up the street, apparently unscathed. The pain eased, though his heart hammered and sweat beaded his brow.

That had been too close for comfort. He could have been killed.

This fatigue and these chest pains are your body's way of warning you that all isn't as it should be.

Jack bowed his head, his hands still gripping the wheel. Dr. Carmichael was right. Jack needed to cut back.

If he didn't want to end up like his grandfather and father before him, he had to face that he could no longer be everything to everyone. It was time to help his family learn to stand on their own feet. Without him.

He'd been wrong not to take his condition seriously.

A FEW DAYS LATER, smoke curled from an oil burner on a shelf in the small but tidy shop. Jack wrinkled his nose, but the smell had a surprising appeal. Sunlight filtered through a window set above shelves of jars, boxes and packets of things he tried not to contemplate. He took in a deep incense-filled breath and rolled his shoulders in an attempt to relax.

"Chamomile." A woman with rosy cheeks smiled from behind a stack of books. "It's good for lots of things, like insomnia and stress."

He nodded, not quite sure how to respond. He'd had his share of both in recent months, among other symptoms. He cleared his throat. "Do you have any books on alternative healing?"

"Sure." She gestured for him to follow her between two book-filled aisles. "Here you go."

He glanced at the assortment of titles. "I want something that's more informational, not a how-to. I'm studying alternative healing methods—what they are."

"I see." She peered at him through narrowed eyes. "This is for your personal use as opposed to research, right?"

Unease rippled through him. "Yes."

Her face split into a smile. "You'll be okay. Spirit gives us only what we can handle."

He laughed, a small strangled sound. Right, he could handle a bad heart and the near certainty of a shortened life. He rubbed his chest as though doing so might relieve the constant pressure there. "Thanks. Can you make a recommendation?"

"Is there a particular type of healing you're interested in?"

"I don't know. I've been to countless doctors. Have been poked, prodded and peered into more times than I care to admit." He stopped.

Why was he telling her this? He hadn't breathed a word to his family. Yet something about the woman put him at ease, loosened his tongue. "A good friend suggested that I look into alternatives. She mentioned several things. I'm not sure where to start."

"Hmm, let's see." She ran her fingers across the

book spines, muttering to herself. "Why don't you try this one?"

He took the book and read the title. "*The Beginner's Guide to Alternative Healing Methods.* I'm certainly a beginner."

He scanned the contents page. "Acupuncture—I tried that last week. Aromatherapy—think I need something with a little more kick to it. Cellular release, etheric pulse—never heard of them. Hypnotherapy, reflexology, reiki—already have an appointment for that. Tantric healing—what's that?"

"Oh, tantra could possibly be the most powerful healing of all."

"Really?" He flipped to the section indicated, then drew back at the picture of a couple entwined in a lovers' embrace. "Are they talking about sexual healing?"

"Like I said, one of the most powerful forms of healing. It's an ancient practice."

He stared at her. "You have to be joking."

"Not at all."

"But…people actually practice this?"

Her eyebrows arched. "Some do. I think I could help you find a local practitioner."

"That's okay. I'll pass." Lifting the book, he said, "I'll take this and read up on some of this other stuff. Maybe I'll find something helpful."

He tamped down on the frustration that threatened

to overwhelm him. He was grasping at straws. What would his family say if they could see him now?

As he followed the woman to the register, he shook his head. His poor mother would be even more confused than he'd already made her when he'd given her the number for a handyman. Jack had tried to ignore her hurt look when he'd insisted he didn't have time to help her any more this week, but the guilt of letting her down and lying to her weighed heavily.

"Is that going to be all for you?" the woman asked.

"That's it."

The issue wasn't so much his time but his need to help his family become more independent. Not to be there for them was just as hard on Jack. He'd been holding them all together for so long, he had to fight the urge to run to the rescue any time his mother needed something fixed or his brother needed advice. They had to learn to stand on their own feet, though.

What would they do if he *wasn't* around?

The woman handed him a bag with the book in it. "Receipt's inside."

"Thank you."

"It would do you a world of good."

"I'm sorry—what would?"

"Tantra."

"Oh, that. I don't know. Seems a little…personal."

"Any kind of healing is going to be tailored for the healee. This type of thing is no different."

"It's hard to imagine hiring a professional for something like that."

"That's not necessarily how it works."

"How does it work then?"

"If you're lucky, you meet a healer and enter into a relationship with her where she imparts her gift to you."

He shook his head. "That takes care of that. I haven't had much luck lately—at least, not what you'd call good."

"But if you met a woman with the healing touch, you'd be open to it?"

"Maybe, but that sounds like something I might need to work my way up to. I'm a novice at all this alternative stuff. I've tried some of it, like I said, and I'm open to other options. Maybe I should try some—" he consulted the book "—hypnotherapy, then perhaps some reflexology. Maybe after all that I'll look at the tantra and see if it seems any more appealing."

"All that takes time. Can you afford to wait?"

A chill shot up his spine. Both his father and grandfather had been struck down in their prime. "I think so."

Her expression was so full of doubt that he had to resist the urge to ask her if she knew something about him he should know. How nuts was that? Of course she didn't know anything. She didn't know him from Jack Sprat.

She leaned across the counter. "Not many know this, but there was a family right here in Miami where all the women inherited the gift of sexual healing."

Again not sure how to respond, he nodded and she said, "I only know because I met the mother and one of the daughters. Must have been at least ten years ago. The daughter was just fourteen at the time and she was this quiet thing. Nothing like her sisters, according to the mother, but there was something about that child. She came in for some feng shui classes—" she gestured to a book leaning against the register "—and she had this presence. I have my own gift. I can tell things about a person. I sensed this powerful energy about her, so I wasn't surprised when the mother, Maggie McClellan, hinted at the family background. They all have it. There's an aunt, too—she comes in from time to time—but you're closer in age to the daughters."

"But even if I was interested in pursuing…that, which I'm not saying I am, what are my chances of meeting any of them?"

Her shoulders shifted beneath her loose cotton dress. "The aunt was in recently, so I believe they're still around. Can't be all that many McClellans in the area. What was that young one's name…Evelyn? No, Erin McClellan, that's it. She was an excellent student of feng shui. I'd be willing to bet she's practicing it somewhere."

"You're suggesting that I look up this woman, strike up a relationship, see if she's interested in sharing her 'gift' with me?"

"Something like that."

He stared at her a moment in disbelief. How could she think such an insane plan would work? Only a desperate man would embark on such a mission.

"One step at a time. Thank you for the book. You have a good day." He headed for the door, but she stopped him halfway there.

"If I were you, I wouldn't take too long with that one-step-at-a-time stuff."

He gave her a half smile, then continued on his way. His chest tightened and he rubbed it. He had time. The one thing he wasn't was a desperate man.

2

"YOU ARE A DESPERATE MAN." Amanda Barnes, Jack's good friend, power walked over a pile of seaweed and regarded him through narrowed eyes. Beyond her, white clouds drifted past a pale blue sky.

He inhaled a breath of salt-tinged air and lengthened his stride to keep pace with her, though the tightening in his chest increased with the effort. "I went there because you told me to go."

"And you do everything I say?"

"Not normally."

"Exactly."

"I'm not saying that I'm even thinking about taking this woman's advice, but I thought you'd have an opinion on tantra."

A wave crashed along the shore beside them and she swerved to avoid the spray, her short blond hair swinging. "I think tantra is a good thing. I don't know much about it except that it involves different positions and meditations."

"Can you see me approaching one of these women? What would I say? 'Please excuse me, miss, but I'm looking for a good sexual healer. I was wondering, might you be available?"

"I'll bet that you could find someone online who would schedule through drop-down menus."

"Is that legal?"

She shrugged. "They're not selling sex. They're selling sexual healing. It's not the same. I'm sure any decent lawyer could establish the difference. Besides, you don't really want to find a healer online. You need to meet her in person. Where did this bookseller say you could find these women?"

"She said one of the daughters' names is Erin McClellan and she'd be around twenty-four and she studied feng shui when she was younger. The woman thought Erin would be practicing it now and I could find her that way."

"You know, I might have heard something about this. What was that last name again?"

"McClellan."

"If this is what I'm thinking, they could be the real thing, truly gifted. Not just tantra, but something…more."

"You've actually heard of them?" he asked.

"I have this friend from yoga class who knows a guy whose roommate's brother may have dated a

McClellan. Don't know if she had any sisters or not, but how many sexual healers can there be?"

He pressed his hand to his chest. "I never said I was looking for one of them."

"Why not?"

Stopping, he stared at her in disbelief. "You said I was desperate for mentioning it."

She circled back beside him and her brown eyes took on a serious light. She nodded to where his hand pressed against his chest. "Your symptoms are getting worse. Look at you, we've hardly gone a quarter of a mile and you're winded. Your best option at this point is surgery that may or may not fix your heart, *if* you survive it. I'd say you're pretty desperate."

He scowled and started walking at a slower pace. His cell phone sounded. Without stopping, he answered it. "Hello?"

"Jack, it's Aunt Rose. Have you got a minute?"

"Sure. What's up?"

"The computer keeps locking up. Do you have time to look at it?"

"Did you ask Bobby?" he asked, slanting Amanda a glance.

"He ran a virus check and did a few other things, but it's still not right. You know he can't fix these things the way you can."

"Okay, I'll try to stop by sometime over the next

few days. I'll call you." He said goodbye, ignoring Amanda's look of censure.

"Jack, you gave in way too easy that time," she chided.

"It's just a computer."

"You can't continue to be everything to every-body. You're so busy taking care of all of them, you're not looking out for number one. You don't need the extra pressure now. What happened to your plan to help them become less dependent on you?"

"I'm easing them into it. At least this time she called Bobby first. They're trying."

Amanda frowned. "Fine, but we still need to get you better."

"Not to worry. There are plenty of other alterna-tive-healing methods I haven't tried. That book listed ones I don't think you know about."

"Did you schedule with that reiki master?"

"I went this morning," he said.

"And?"

"It was very peaceful and relaxing, but I didn't feel the earth move."

"It's not like that."

"She said the reiki would continue to work for a while longer and that my energies were more balanced, whatever that means." He glanced at her. "She said my heart chakra—some kind of energy-center thing—was closed or deunified or something and that was partly why I was having trouble."

He spread his arms in appeal. "I don't get all this energy talk. Maybe I should stick to conventional medicine. I have a physical defect in my arterial valve. How will balancing my energies or channeling some life force or whatever she was doing help that?"

"It's all connected. What affects the emotional body impacts the physical body, as well as the etheric and so forth," Amanda said.

He frowned at her. The woman was nuts. Why was he listening to her?

She raised her hands. "All I'm saying is that unresolved emotional issues manifest as physical illness."

"Besides the fact that all that mumbo jumbo sounds a little flaky, this is more a defect than an illness."

"Still, it's worth a shot."

"You think I should find one of these McClellan women and strike up a relationship?" he asked.

"It beats hiring a sexual healer off the Internet."

A sail moved along the horizon. A gull screeched overhead. The hammering of his heart echoed in his ears. He stopped again. "You think it might work?"

She wiped a bead of perspiration from her forehead. "This woman healed my friend's friend's roommate's brother of emphysema. His doctor took before-and-after X-rays of his lungs. It was unheard of. The whole thing was documented in some obscure medical journal. And he wasn't the only one. Apparently she has a following of men she's healed. They all adore her and each swears she's healed them in one way or another."

"You sure you didn't read that in the *Enquirer?*"

Her eyebrows arched. "Yes, I'm sure. She healed him, Jack. You have to find her or one of her sisters, if that's the case. Maybe we can Google the one who does feng shui."

"Google her?"

"If she's practicing feng shui, I'll bet she has a Web site."

"And what would I say to her if we were to find her?"

"You'd just introduce your charming self and let nature run its course."

"I don't know. The whole thing sounds ludicrous."

"Hold on." She pulled her flip phone from her pocket, opened it, then punched a few buttons.

"I'll bet my friend George can get some information. He's still good friends with— Oh, here's his voice mail…Hey, George, it's Amanda. Listen, I'm trying to get the scoop on the woman who healed that guy's emphysema. Was her last name McClellan? You know the one who has the gift of sexual healing? Can you talk to your friend and see if he can get an update on her and her family from his roommate's brother? I was hoping you could help me locate her or one of her sisters if she has any. Okay, so call me when you have something. Thanks, I owe you."

She hung up and smiled at him. "There, we'll have you all set in no time."

A feeling of apprehension settled over him. God, he *was* a desperate man.

SUNLIGHT FELL THROUGH a skylight onto Erin's desk in her design studio. She sighed and flipped through the stack of invoices she'd been ignoring for the past week. There was no more putting it off. It was time to balance her accounts.

A whisper of movement sounded and she started, then stared. A blond stranger stepped into the sunlight spilling around her desk. He was tall and lean, his eyes dark and intense.

Her heart pounded. "Goodness, you scared me."

He gestured toward the front. "Oh, sorry. The bell jingled, but you must not have heard." Moving forward, he extended his hand. "I'm Jack Langston and I'm guessing you're Erin McClellan."

She rose, taking his hand as she moved around the desk. A shock of warmth spread through her at the contact. "Yes, I'm Erin. Guess I've been a little too absorbed in balancing my accounts. Or at least trying to." She laughed, the sound seeming strained to her own ears.

He seemed to fill the splash of sunlight as though he was part of it—an angel sent to taunt her with his beauty. "It's a pleasure to meet you, Mr. Langston."

"The pleasure's mine. Please call me Jack. I've heard so much about you."

"You have? Then do you mind if I ask who referred you?"

"I didn't catch her name. She owns a little shop down in Coconut Grove. It's called the Emperor's Attic."

"The Emperor's Attic?" Unease gripped her.

"I believe she was the owner. She's certainly worked there a long time. She spoke highly of you…and your family."

"My family? What did she say about my family?" Her mind raced. She hadn't been there in ages, but her unconventional relatives no doubt still frequented the metaphysical bookstore.

Jack straightened. "Mostly she talked about how well known you are for your work with feng shui."

"But you said she talked about my family." A faint roaring sounded in her ears. She tried to breathe, but it felt as if a weight pressed her chest.

"Isn't this a family business?"

"No, this is *my* interior-design business. I don't

work with feng shui anymore." A myriad of emotions swamped her. She leaned against her desk to steady herself. What was wrong with her?

"You don't?" He frowned. "Why not?"

"I've decided to pursue a more mainstream clientele."

"Mainstream?" A note of disbelief colored his voice.

"Mr. Langston, I'm not sure what you've heard about me or my family, but I assure you I run a very respectable business here." Who was this man to question her in this way?

"I don't doubt that, Ms. McClellan, but I don't see anything disrespectable about feng shui. I'm no expert, but it seems quite a good number of upstanding citizens swear by it."

"I'm not saying there's anything wrong with it. I have simply chosen not to practice that type of design anymore. I find my business has picked up significantly since I decided to go with the more conventional mode of interior design."

"But you would take on a job for a paying client if he wanted you to use your knowledge of feng shui?" He moved a step closer.

The tumult of emotions clamored inside her. She pressed her lips together to keep from crying out. *He* caused this tangle of feelings. Was this the empathic nature her family spoke of?

Well, they could have it.

"Are you such a client?" she asked.

He met her steady gaze. "Yes, I believe I am."

"You're saying you're interested in feng shui?"

"That's right. I have a condo on the intercoastal. It needs—" he gestured lamely "—some of that stuff."

"Feng shui is more a philosophy than a collection of 'stuff.'"

"Right. I need your expertise on how to bring that philosophy into my home."

"And are you familiar with it then, Mr. Langston?"

"Jack."

"Okay, Jack, what do you know about feng shui?"

"It's the philosophy of…how energy—" he wiggled his hand through the air "—moves through space…and how you can arrange a living area…to promote harmony, balance and well-being." He smiled triumphantly.

A shock—a connection—ran between them. She stood for a moment, not breathing as the turmoil inside her subsided and a feeling of well-being wrapped around her. She fisted her hands, fighting the outrageous urge to touch him.

Then she glanced away. Whoever he was, the feelings he stirred in her were anything but normal. "I'm afraid I can't help you."

"Why not?" He stepped even closer to her.

For an instant she thought he might grab her. A thrill shot through her and she chastised herself for the unwanted reaction. "My schedule is full. I'm not currently accepting new clients."

"Maybe if you saw my place, you'd feel inspired. It's a great condo."

"No doubt."

"And if I wanted to hire you for some regular interior-design work, would you be available?"

She stared at him a long moment, a strange sense of longing filling her. But he'd come from the Emperor's Attic. He was interested in feng shui. He knew a little about her family.

And she was attracted to him.

"I've already told you that my schedule is full," she finally said.

Disappointment flashed in his eyes. "Very well, Erin." He handed her one of his business cards. "In case you change your mind."

She took his card and extended her hand. "Thank you for stopping by." His hand was warm and firm. The odd sense of well-being blanketed her. Her chest tightened with regret. "I'm sorry to disappoint you."

"Are you?"

She let go of his hand, but the connection stretched between them. "Yes, Jack, I am."

He nodded toward the card in her hand. "You know how to reach me."

She refrained from comment as he turned and walked away.

Several hours later, Erin rubbed her eyes, then focused again on the numbers in the spreadsheet. Damn, she hadn't realized she was cutting things so close this month.

And she'd turned away a paying customer.

Thoughts of Jack Langston assailed her, as they had numerous times since he'd left. It would be best to stay away from that one. The man was anything but conventional. Her life had already been one unconventional mess after another.

While Erin was growing up, her mother had dragged her and her sisters from lover to lover, home to home. The rootless existence had taken its toll on Erin. In her teens, she had delved into feng shui in an attempt to bring some order to the standard chaos of their temporary living arrangements, but no sooner would she make a place livable then they'd be off to Maggie's next lover.

When Erin had been old enough, she'd escaped to live with her sisters. They had stayed in one place, but with Nikki's night creepers and Tess's minions, though, Erin had traded one circus for another. More than anything now she needed *normal,* and Jack did *not* fit that bill.

The bell on her door jingled and she jumped, her heart speeding the way it had when Jack Langston had appeared beside her desk earlier.

She groaned inwardly as Tess headed toward her, their oldest sister, Nikki, in tow. Both bore looks of determination. Erin braced herself as they stopped, arms crossed, before her.

"Okay, miss, it's quitting time. You're coming with us." Tess glanced at Nikki for confirmation.

"That's right, Erin. We're stealing you away. No arguments," Nikki said. "We haven't seen enough of you lately and Mason and Dylan are both tied up, so Tess and I are on our own for the night. The timing couldn't be better."

Erin eyed them warily. "Better for what?"

"Ladies' night." Tess grabbed Erin's purse from the back of her chair. "Let's go. If we hurry, we can make happy hour."

"Wait a minute. Since when are the two of you so anxious to hit happy hour? Nikki, you hate clubbing. And Tess, you'd be asking for trouble by setting foot in a bar. What is this really about?"

"We want to spend some time with you. Why does it have to be about anything more than that?" Nikki's eyes filled with censure.

"I don't feel like going to a bar. Why don't we go to a nice restaurant instead? Someplace we can actually hear each other." Erin said.

"Okay." Tess slung Erin's purse over her own shoulder and headed for the door. "Let's go to that little place in South Beach."

"Wait, come back with my purse." Erin hurried after her. "What place in South Beach?"

"That place that Josh discovered that he likes so well."

"What place? You are talking about a restaurant, right?"

"Come on. We'll have fun. When was the last time we had a girls' night out?" Nikki asked.

Unease rippled along Erin's spine. Something was fishy about this whole thing. She dug in her heels, but Tess pushed through the door. Groaning, Erin followed.

3

TWENTY MINUTES LATER Erin stared up at the neon sign in disbelief. "B.E.D? What kind of place is this?"

"It's the hottest club in Miami. You really should get out more." Tess moved around the long line outside the club and waved three VIP passes at the doorman, who motioned her through the large double doors.

"I thought we were going to a nice restaurant." Erin raised her voice over the music pounding from inside.

Nikki shrugged. "Tess set her mind on this, and you know how she is. There was no talking her out of it. You're right about one thing. Mason will blow a gasket when he hears she came here. Look, they're already starting to flock."

Indeed, Tess had already drawn a small group of male admirers as she stopped to wait for her sisters. Erin folded her arms. "I'm not doing this."

"Yes, you are." Tess turned to Erin and looped her arm through hers. "Here she is, boys, my sister Erin. Who's going to buy her a drink?"

"Tess." Erin glared first at the men, who dropped back, then at her sister as Tess dragged her through another set of doors.

Green and pink lights flashed throughout a cavernous area swarming with hopeful singles. Erin blinked through the smoky haze. "Good God, are those beds?"

"Complete with plush pillows." One of the men from Tess's flock smiled at her, his teeth unnaturally white—or was that the fluorescent lighting? "Shall we?"

"Shall we what?" Erin asked.

He gestured toward the nearest bed, where several people lay sprawled in various positions, some propped on what indeed appeared to be plush pillows. One couple's limbs were so entwined, she couldn't tell where one ended and the other started.

Gritting her teeth, she turned to Tess. "What the hell are we doing here?"

"Don't get upset." Nikki stepped between the two. "Let's sit and see if we can't have some fun. It isn't like we've never been clubbing before. What's everyone drinking?"

Erin gestured around her. "This isn't a club. It's a meat market."

"You want to know what tonight is?" Tess asked, her eyes wide. "This is an intervention."

Erin blinked. "What?"

"You've been moping around too much lately." Nikki shooed a man over and made room for the three of them on the bed. "Come on, sit beside me. Look at all the lovely men."

"Pick one," Tess said. "It's time to get back on the horse."

Erin glared at her.

Nikki touched Erin's arm. "We're just worried about you since that thing with Ryan."

"I have written off men," Erin said as she perched on the edge of the massive mattress.

"Good thing we planned this intervention then." Tess signaled a waitress over.

Her eyes filled with concern, Nikki leaned toward Erin while Tess ordered drinks for all of them. "Sweetie, I know you've been a little unhappy lately, but there's no reason for such drastic action. You can't swear off men. You're a McClellan. You'll put Aunt Sophie in her grave, not to mention what Maggie will say when she hears about it."

"This has nothing to do with Aunt Sophie or our mother," Erin said. "I don't expect the two of you to understand."

Tess sank onto one of the pillows. "I get it. You jumped into the love arena and got hurt, so you're hesitant to get back in there. Completely understandable, but it'll all work out. This kind of thing happens all the time. Even to us. Right, Nikki?"

Nikki nodded. "But we worked through it and so can you, Erin."

"I hate to disappoint the two of you, but there isn't anyone for me to work things through with. And there isn't going to be." Erin's gaze drifted over the cluster of men standing a few feet away, waiting for the smallest encouragement.

"It doesn't have to be like that," Nikki said. "All we wanted was to let you know that we think you're making a mistake. Maybe this isn't the right time or place for you to find a great guy. Maybe you'll find him in a nice restaurant or maybe one of these days he'll waltz through your shop door. The point is that you should never give up. It'll be worth it, and in time you'll laugh about swearing off men."

Maybe one of these days he'll waltz through your shop door.

Nikki's words sent goose bumps running up Erin's arms. Hadn't a great guy walked through her door earlier that day? And what had she done? She'd sent him on his way. "It wouldn't matter."

"What do you mean?" Tess asked.

The memory of Jack Langston's intent gaze warmed Erin. When he had looked at her today, it had been as if he had really seen her in a way no one ever had. He'd been like some otherworldly phantom with his sudden appearance.

She let her gaze drift again over the hopefuls: one built like a linebacker, with vivid green eyes; one as toned and buff as any bodybuilder, an intelligence in his eyes that might have intrigued her in the past; and one with a bright smile hinting at a playfulness that might have appealed to her at another time.

A time before meeting Jack.

"I don't know how to explain," she finally said.

Nikki squeezed her hand. "Try, hon. Is it about the gift?"

She should just tell them. But how could she say she rejected the gift and all it stood for without making them feel she rejected them? She'd been hard-pressed to spend time with her sisters lately. She couldn't shake her disappointment that they'd fallen in with their mother's ways.

Finally she said. "It doesn't matter. I appreciate what you're trying to do here, but I really don't want a man in my life right now."

Nikki nodded. "Well, we had to try. Maybe you just need a little time."

Time. Would that make any difference? If only she hadn't had to turn Jack away. He'd been interested in more than a feng shui consultation. Her empathic nature might not be as well developed as either of her sisters', but she could tell that much.

"Okay, so if you're not going to dance with any of the men here, the least we can do is enjoy our drinks." Tess passed them umbrella-topped glasses. She lifted her glass high. "To love and finding it in unexpected places."

"To love." Nikki clinked her glass first to Tess's, then Erin's.

Erin nodded, then took a tentative sip, a sense of loss filling her. To love? How had Typhoid Mary fared in that arena?

"HI, THOMAS, IS AUNT SOPHIE here?" Erin peered past her longtime family friend the following afternoon as she stood in the open door of her aunt's house.

She hadn't had any appointments that morning and had finished packing her apartment. Her new home was ready. The movers would arrive in the morning.

"She and your mother are in Fort Lauderdale at a seminar."

"Oh." Disappointment filled her. If this was anything like previous healing seminars they'd been to, it would keep them tied up for the rest of the day. "I just thought I'd visit."

"What am I, chopped liver?"

"I would love to visit with you." She laughed in spite of herself.

Thomas had always been able to lighten her mood. Too bad Maggie hadn't ever hooked up with him. He'd have made a better father to Erin and her sisters than any of the men who had drifted in and out of her mother's life.

His smile warmed her as he led her back to the brightly lit kitchen. He motioned her to the table and headed for the coffeepot. "I was just taking a break."

"What are you working on?"

"Stopped by to finish some lighting in Maggie's new studio. It helps her…the light is…getting to be a problem."

Her throat tightened. She still struggled with accepting the fact that her mother was slowly going blind. "So how is she?"

"She's a trooper, that's for sure."

"Maybe I shouldn't have come. I don't want to interrupt your work."

He placed a cup of coffee in front of her and sat down across from her with his own. "Nonsense. Take a break with me. You didn't come here to talk about Maggie."

Guilt swamped her. "I do want to talk about her. I'm concerned about her, Thomas."

"She knows that, but she doesn't want you to be.

She's adamant that we all keep the status quo. She's even continuing to paint. We've set up her studio so she can find everything by feel when the time comes. The other day she tried a practice run with a blindfold."

Erin's stomach twisted at the thought of Maggie painting blindfolded. "She can't be serious about continuing with her painting. Not after…"

"She is." He shrugged. "At least for now. I think it's important to support her in whatever she's doing to deal with this."

"But it seems so…hopeless."

"Not to your mother, and the last thing she needs from any of us is discouragement." He poured sugar into his cup. "The best thing you can do for her is to not show her how worried you are."

She nodded.

"So?" He leaned toward her. "I live close enough that I know you girls show up on your aunt's doorstep when you have some trouble to chew over with her."

"Compared to Maggie, how can I complain?"

"I'm all ears."

"I'm having a little trouble with all this. You know, the healing stuff, the McClellan gift."

"You mean the sexual healing."

Heat tinged her cheeks. "Is it wrong for me to want to have a normal life? To not feel that I need to have a man around?"

"I've heard some of this—about your plan to move off on your own and give up men. They're all in an uproar, aren't they?"

"I knew when I told Nikki and Tess that I was moving word would spread."

"You didn't need that big place all to yourself. Makes sense. When's the big day?"

"Tomorrow. I don't have much. It shouldn't be too bad." She sipped her coffee. "Nikki and Tess dragged me out to pick up men last night. It was a total disaster."

"You really want to be all on your own?"

"Yes, I don't want a man in my life. I don't need one."

He shrugged and drank from his mug. "I think a girl's entitled to date or not date. They'll get over it eventually."

"Exactly. I choose if and when I date, just like I choose whether or not to work with any client in particular."

"Do you pick and choose your clients?"

Her stomach tightened. Why had she mentioned that? "Well, I've always been grateful for any clients that come my way. I've never turned one down...until yesterday."

"You turned down a client?"

"He wanted a consultation on feng shui. I don't

do that anymore. I have the right to pursue a more conventional career, don't I?"

"Of course you do, Erin, but since when did you decide that you didn't like feng shui anymore?"

"Since I decided to get serious about establishing myself in interior design. My business has really picked up."

"Enough for you to turn away a potential client?"

"I'm making more, but I seem to be spending more, too." She shifted in her seat. "He can find someone else to help him."

"Sure he can, but no one does feng shui like you do, hon."

"Like I did."

"So you plan to live a conventional, man-free life."

"Exactly. What's the problem with that? What can I do to get my family to respect my decision?"

"I don't know." He scratched the back of his neck. "Your personal life is one thing, but it seems a little unconventional, not to mention unprofessional, to turn down a paying customer. It's not the way I'd advise you to run your business."

He was right. It was bad business to turn away a customer, especially during a lean month. Yet the thought of working with Jack Langston gave her a distinctly disquieted feeling. She was just too attracted to the man.

Thomas leaned back and cocked his head. "It's a guess, but I'd say this potential customer was just such a young man to test your new no-man vow."

She stared at him a moment. How could he possibly know? "I never said I wouldn't have men as clients."

"But you turned down this man."

"He wanted feng shui."

"Is that all he wanted?"

"Yes. He didn't come on to me, if that's what you're thinking." Her cheeks warmed. Jack may not have come on to her, but her gut told her he had wanted to.

"But you wanted him to, and that was a problem for some reason."

"I did not."

"Oh, okay, my mistake." He carried his cup to the sink. "Would you like more coffee?"

"No, thank you." Erin stared at her half-finished cup. "I'd better let you get back to work. I need to head to the shop myself."

"Okay, sweetheart, I'll let Sophie know you stopped by."

She moved beside him. "Thanks, Thomas, I enjoyed the coffee."

"Don't be afraid to embrace who you are, Erin. You come from an extraordinary family. Each of you is very different and you should accept and celebrate those differences, just like you should celebrate the similarities."

A short laugh burst from her. "Right, like I have so much in common with the rest of them."

"I'm betting you have more in common than you realize. Maybe it's just tucked away a little bit, but it's there."

"You think so?"

He walked her to the door. "Yes, I do. No reason not to."

"Thanks, Thomas." She kissed his cheek as he held the door. "Tell Maggie I'll give her a call."

She headed to her car, his words rolling through her mind.

I'd say this potential customer was just such a young man to test your new no-man vow.

He'd hit the mark. Maybe if she had a little more in common with her family then she wouldn't have to close herself off from romantic relationships.

She slipped behind her wheel and sighed. Her lack of the gift was one thing she couldn't bring herself to celebrate. It wasn't fair. Nikki had Dylan and Tess had Mason. Even Maggie had Thomas in a way.

Erin glanced at the house. Why was it that Thomas and her mother had never hooked up romantically? The two were like intricate pieces to a puzzle. One would never be whole without the other.

Thomas loved her mother. Everyone knew that, probably even Maggie. Was that why she'd never encouraged a sexual relationship with him? Did she fear that once they became lovers she would be destined to move on and leave him behind, the way she had with all her past lovers?

The thought comforted Erin in an odd way. Was it possible she could have a Thomas in her life? She pulled out Jack's card from her wallet.

Could Jack be her Thomas?

She pressed her hand to her face. One thing was for certain—her bottom line was suffering too much to make this decision. She'd been foolish to turn down a paying job.

Simple, clear fonts accentuated Jack's card. Information-Security Investigator. Some kind of techie, no doubt. She stared at the number until it blurred. Would he be willing to settle for a standard interior-design job? She'd never know if she didn't call him.

With her heart thudding, she carefully pressed his number on her cell phone. His phone rang once, twice, then a third time. His soft baritone vibrated along the line, caressing her ear. "Jack Langston here."

"Jack, good afternoon, this is Erin McClellan. You stopped by my design studio yesterday."

"Erin," he said, his voice lightening. "What a happy surprise. How are you?"

Her pulse pounded in her ears and she was sixteen again, asking Dale Stone to the Sadie Hawkins dance. "I'm doing well. Did I get you at a good time?"

"Perfect, I'm on my way to a meeting."

"Oh, what kind of meeting?" She rolled her eyes at her own evident stalling.

"The usual. Helping some corporate information-security team figure out how their system was breached. They usually have their own protocol in these cases, but they tend to miss things. That's when they call me."

She bit her lip. "Oh, that must be really interesting."

"I enjoy it. Keeps me busy."

She nodded, at a loss as to how to continue. She was an idiot for calling.

"So not that I'm complaining, but I'm sure you have a reason for this call."

"Yes, of course." Her face warmed. "I just…I was thinking I may have been…" She inhaled a deep breath, then took the plunge. "My schedule has cleared some and I was wondering if you still needed a designer?"

A long silence hummed across the phone. She frowned. "Jack?"

"Hello, Erin? Can you hear me?"

"Yes, I hear you."

"Sorry, I lost you for a minute."

"Oh, I was saying that my schedule has cleared—"

"Yes, I heard that. That's great news. I would love it if you could work me in."

"Great." She let out a shaky breath.

"I respect your feelings in that you favor interior design over feng shui and I think we can work something out."

"I'm sure we can."

"How about this? We'll start with a more traditional theme, one in keeping with your interior-design methods, but you'll work in the feng shui as you see fit. Surely that can be done, can't it?"

Her stomach tightened. "I suppose it could."

"My guess is that the two would complement each other."

She pursed her lips. "They're really two different philosophies."

"Which is what makes you such a unique choice. I can't imagine where else I could find a designer who is also first in the fine art of feng shui."

"Not everyone has the same appreciation for it. I always felt it was important to strengthen my training with the more well-known aspects of interior design."

"And it looks like I'm to benefit. I'll have the best of both worlds."

"I wouldn't claim to be the best, Jack, but I will give you my best effort."

"Which is all it takes to be the best."

She sat a moment in silence. Had she let him talk her into giving him a feng shui consultation? "I'll e-mail you the standard contract."

"That would be really great, Erin. I can't tell you how excited I am that you've agreed to take me on as a client."

She couldn't help but smile. "I'm looking forward to it."

"Great," he said. "Why don't you come by my condo, say around seven?"

"Tonight?"

"Yes, is that okay? I'm anxious to get started."

She paused for a few seconds, assessing. "I'll be there."

4

"IT'S...AMAZING." ERIN let her gaze drift over the open space of Jack's main living area.

Sunlight slanted low through floor-to-ceiling windows and spilled over the white tile floor. A sparse assortment of eclectic furniture circled a worn area rug. Bare walls bordered the room. The scent of roasting meat and spices filled the air.

Jack shrugged. "You can see why I need you."

In spite of her reservations about this project and this particular man, excitement coursed through her. Here in the comfort of his own home he appeared relaxed and even more striking in khakis and a light blue shirt. He glanced at her and caught her staring. Her pulse quickened as she glanced away and stepped farther into the room, focusing on her surroundings.

"It's not so bad. I've definitely seen worse." At least it was clean, in a stark kind of way. "This is almost like a blank canvas. It's easier to picture what we might do with it."

She sidestepped around him and pulled out her notebook. "Which rooms are you interested in having me redo for you?"

"Oh, here." He moved to a desk tucked into one corner of the room. "I printed out the contract you e-mailed. I filled in all the pertinent details." He handed her two copies. "It's signed."

"Great." She scanned the pages, her gaze settling briefly on his bold signature scrawled across the bottom. "It all looks in order." She flipped back a page, then glanced at him. "You want me to do the entire house?"

"Yep, the entire house." He gestured in a sweeping motion. "The rest is about the same."

"Okay." She hesitated, her pen poised. Was she really ready to take him on as a client?

Seems a little unconventional, not to mention unprofessional, to turn down a paying customer.

She signed one of the contracts, then handed it to him. "Redesigning the entire house will take some time."

"Time isn't an issue." His gaze traced her face, drawing warmth to her cheeks. "In fact," he continued, "the longer the better."

"Oh." Her breath caught and her skin warmed more. She responded so readily to just one look from him.

What had she signed herself up for?

He handed her a check. "I believe this covers your standard deposit as outlined in the contract."

"Yes, thank you. This will do nicely." She tucked the check into her purse. "Well, then, why don't we start in this room?" she said, holding her notebook before her like a shield and taking a deep breath of the delicious-smelling air. "I'd like to ask you a few questions." Her stomach growled. What was the man cooking? She was absolutely starving.

She perched on the edge of a love seat with over-size throw pillows. He settled in a chair beside her. "Shoot."

"What do you use this room for?"

"That's a good question. I don't really know. I don't use it that much. I'm not home but to sleep mostly. I guess that's why I've never done much with the place."

"Really? Where do you spend all your time?" She couldn't help asking, intrigued in spite of herself. "How does a…systems information-security…person…spend his time?"

"Information-security investigator." His shoulders rippled in an easy shrug. "I spend a lot of time on-site, reading logs, checking configurations or setting them up, depending on the current job. The smart clients hire me before they experience a breach. Figuring out how a system's been breached—that's different with every job."

"So you're a computer geek."

His eyebrows arched. "I've been called worse. I prefer techie, but geek is probably more accurate."

"You're not what I'd call a geek." Embarrassment swept through her. Why had she admitted that? "No glasses or pocket protectors."

"I try to stay away from the more obvious indicators."

A smile curved her lips. "Back to business."

"*If* I spent more time here, I guess this is where I'd entertain my guests, should I have any."

"Entertainment." She jotted a few notes. "And is that more formal entertaining or casual?"

He laughed. "Honey, there's not a formal bone in my body."

"Okay, casual. Do you have any preferences as far as design?"

He held her gaze. "All I can say is that I know what I want when I see it."

"And do you see anything you want?"

Desire shone in his eyes. The connection they'd shared in her shop sprang to life, humming between them. "Yes, ma'am. I do."

She looked away. "In the room, I mean. Do you want to keep any of this?"

"Oh." He glanced around. "I'll leave that up to you. We could sell some of this to a thrift shop or give it to charity."

She glanced thoughtfully at the few furnishings in the room. "I like the desk. It may be salvageable, though we might want to move it to another room. Keep this more open."

His smile crinkled the corners of his eyes. "Right, that's a feng shui thing, isn't it? I knew you wouldn't be able to help working some of that in."

"It's a perfectly acceptable design principle to balance your open and filled spaces."

He nodded, seemingly satisfied. "Why don't I give you the grand tour? That way you can get an idea of which are the keepers and where you might want to put everything."

"Okay." She rose to follow him, bumping into him as they both turned toward the hall. Her hand collided with his chest. Her heart raced. "Excuse me."

As she stepped away from him, he gestured for her to precede him. "Let me introduce you to my humble abode."

Smiling, Jack moved down the wide hall behind Erin, mesmerized by the gentle sway of her hips and the curve of her ass. She was a little thing, almost doll-like with her porcelain skin and wide eyes. If he remembered correctly, that doll his sister Stacey had dragged around for years when she was a child had just the same tint of green in her glass eyes.

He shook his head. Stacey would have liked Erin. Somehow he just knew it.

"It's not so humble." Erin turned to him, then made another note or two in her notebook. "Look at all the wide spaces, the detail. I'd give anything for that crown molding."

She stopped in the archway leading into the kitchen. He nodded as he stood behind her. This was his favorite room in the house. Wide garden windows overlooked a spacious backyard and rimmed an area meant for cooking. Stainless-steel appliances and glass-fronted cabinets added a contemporary feel. An empty breakfast nook sat off to one side.

She turned again to him, her smile lighting her face, and his stomach did a little flip-flop at the excitement in her eyes. She spread her arms wide. "Now *this* is a kitchen."

"I'm glad you like it."

"It's wonderful. A cook's dream. My aunt Sophie would camp out in here. We'd never see her. You must love it." She moved into the room and ran her hand along the island counter separating the breakfast nook from the rest of the kitchen.

"It's what sold me on this place. Do you cook?" he asked.

"Enough to get by. Evidently not like you, though, if that wonderful smell is any indication. Do you cook often or did I just catch you on a good night?"

"I like puttering around in the kitchen. I can whip up a decent meal." When his father died and his mother hadn't been able to cope, Jack had learned to manage the household. Cooking was just part of it. It had been a matter of survival.

"You don't have to convince me. My mouth's watering. What is that?"

"Meat loaf. There's plenty. You'd be more than welcome to join me."

"Oh…" Pink suffused her cheeks. "I wasn't fishing for an invitation. I wouldn't dream of intruding. It just smells so good and I don't know of many men, at least single men, who cook—not that I'd really know, but—"

"Erin, would you please have dinner with me? If I had been thinking clearly, I would have asked you earlier when we scheduled for tonight. I have some mashed potatoes and a salad, too. It's not much. The meat loaf won't be ready for another half hour, but I would love for you to join me."

"Do you cook like this every night? I mean, a full meal for yourself?"

"Not really every night. I eat the leftovers for a day

or two afterward. Sometimes I'll make a big batch of something, then freeze whatever is left. Once I lived off a batch of chili for three weeks." And often, still, he took food to his mother's, but that was going to end.

"You didn't get tired of it?"

He let his gaze again drift over her. From head to toe, there wasn't anything about her that he could find fault with. "When I find something I like, I don't mind sticking with it."

She looked away and he could have hit himself. There he went again—open mouth, spill guts. Why was it that way with her?

"Actually it's easier to cook in bulk. Since I'm by myself, it doesn't really matter what I make. As long as it fills my stomach, I can eat just about anything. I generally work at the computer while I eat. That's not so great for the keyboard, but it kills two birds with one stone."

Her gaze softened. "Sounds a little lonely."

He shrugged. "Hadn't really thought of it that way. Never bothers me."

"My family takes mealtime pretty seriously. Always lots of food. No distractions like work. Dinner is family time."

"Ah, well, home is a different story altogether. My mother was the same way. My sister used to sneak books to the table, hiding them in her lap." He smiled, remembering the old days when they'd all been together. "Only Stacey could ever get away with that. If one of us guys were to try it, we'd be dead meat."

"Stacey is your sister?"

He straightened. Why had he been running off at the mouth like that again? "Uh, yes."

"And you have brothers?"

"Just one brother, Bobby. He lives in Boca, near my mother and her sister. They live in this big house they can hardly keep up with. Between the two of us, we look after them." He closed his mouth. He didn't seem to have any control over the personal information that spewed from him.

He pushed on before she thought to ask more about his family. "So are you joining me for dinner or am I doomed to spend another evening spilling crumbs all over my keyboard?"

She bit her lip, and he couldn't tear his gaze from the contrast of her white teeth against her pink lips. The woman had a mouth meant to entice. Her brow furrowed. "Jack, I'm sure you don't mean anything by this, but I want to clarify that it's a policy of mine not to date clients."

It was his turn for his face to warm. "Sure, I understand absolutely and couldn't agree more. Just offering to fill your stomach. We can talk business the whole time if that'll make you feel better."

The clock on the wall ticked. The meat loaf sizzled in the oven. At last she nodded. "Guess I could come to your keyboard's rescue."

"My keyboard? What about poor, lonely me?"

She cocked her head. "Somehow you don't seem so lonely to me."

"Well, I'm not." He shrugged. "I stay way too busy for that." Or he kept himself too busy to think about it. With her standing beside him, close enough to touch, an evening alone with his computer didn't seem all that appealing.

Her eyes took on a teasing light. "Now if we get this place fixed up for entertaining, you'll have to promise me you'll actually use it for that."

The only person he felt like entertaining at any time in the near future was the woman before him. "Maybe, but only if you'll come play hostess for me. That stuff is way beyond me."

"That'll entail an additional fee."

Her soft scent wrapped around him and it was all he could do to keep from touching her. "I'm sure we can work something out."

That becoming pink again flushed her cheeks. Her gaze fell to his lips and her body swayed forward, while his pulse strummed. Then she straightened, all business, her notebook pressed close to her chest. "First things first. Shall we continue the tour?"

"Certainly." Disappointment swirled through him, but he tamped it down.

This time he led her through the dining room, where they stopped briefly, then on to the small sunroom before they moved toward the bedrooms. What the hell was he doing anyway? So far he was making a mess of winging this ridiculous plan he'd let Amanda talk him into.

What had he been thinking? That Erin McClellan would take one look at him and fall swooning into his arms? Even if she had, then what? They'd have some strange sexual-healing relationship?

What the hell was that anyway?

"These are wonderful frames." The fascination in Erin's voice drew him back to the present—to the woman he'd hired to redesign his home.

It had been an impulsive plan, born of desperation, that had driven him to her shop. When she'd closed up about her family and spouted her conventional leanings, he hadn't known what else to do. Asking her point-blank to enter into a sexual-healing relationship with him had been out of the question. Of course, he hadn't considered a no-dating policy when he'd signed that contract.

At least she'd agreed to stay for dinner.

He groaned inwardly. Why had he made meat loaf, for Pete's sake? Why couldn't he have asked her *out* to dinner? She would have turned him down, but at least he wouldn't have seemed like some dorky Suzy Homemaker.

"Jack?" Her green gaze pinned him and he forced his attention to the photographs on the dresser in his guest room. "We should keep these frames. They're beautiful. Antiques, right?"

"Sure. Whatever you say."

She set the picture she'd picked up down beside its comrades. "Is this your family?"

He nodded as she indicated the figures in the photographs. He'd forgotten about the pictures. Stacey had brought them over years ago. She'd claimed this as her room when he'd bought the condo and she'd run here whenever she'd needed to get away from home.

Christ, he hadn't changed a thing in all the time she'd been gone.

"This must be your sister. She's gorgeous. She favors you."

He nodded, his throat tight. Damn, he hadn't expected to get choked up. It had been almost seven years now. The ache in his throat intensified. Shit. He was going to lose it if they stayed in here. "Let's move on."

5

WITHOUT WAITING FOR Erin's response, Jack swung toward the door, but her hand on his arm stayed him. He turned to her. The compassion in her eyes stopped him cold. His throat burned.

Her eyes were luminous, brimming. "You lost her, didn't you?"

The room blurred. He nodded, confusion swirling around him like a cloud. He'd grieved for his sister years ago in the quiet of night. Alone.

Why this now?

"I'm so sorry." Her voice, soft as a caress, stroked the first tear down his cheek.

"Damn." He did turn then and huffed out a breath. What the hell kind of impression was he making? He'd never cried in front of anyone like this, especially not in front of a woman.

"I—" He cleared his throat. "It's been years. She was just sixteen." He shook his head and straightened, composing himself before he faced her. "I'm not sure what brought that on."

Her hand smoothed up his arm, sending ripples of awareness through him. He clamped his own hand over hers to still her, suddenly feeling very out of control of his emotions again. This woman had the oddest effect on him.

Could this be part of her gift?

"It's okay. I didn't mean to pry." She dropped her hand. "Grief has a way of sneaking up on you. Best to let it out when it does." She frowned. "I should go."

"No." He grabbed her arm, then stared at his hand, surprised he'd done so, but the thought of her leaving sent a sense of loss shooting through him. Regardless of what kind of effect she had on him, he wasn't yet ready for her to go.

He released her. "Excuse me. We're not through and I'm not letting you slide on that dinner. I made a ton of meat loaf. You've got to help me eat it."

A hesitant smile curved her lips. In that moment he thought there wasn't anything he wouldn't do for one of her smiles. Damn, the woman had the most enchanting way about her.

Her eyes shone. "Okay, but you're just lucky I have a soft spot for meat loaf."

"I'll have to remember that."

"There's gravy, too, I hope."

"Meat loaf and mashed potatoes without gravy? What do I look like—some kind of freak? Never mind. Don't answer that."

She laughed, and the sound trickled up his spine and filled him with warmth, but her gaze was anything but playful. "No, Jack Langston, you do not look like a freak to me."

He couldn't resist it anymore. He reached for a lock of her hair, rubbing it briefly between his fingers before tucking it behind her ear. The simple act sent adrenaline shooting through him.

Truly the woman had magic in her. How else could he explain this quickening—this lightening of his spirit—with just a look, a touch from her? The need to know her filled him.

"Tell me about your family," he asked.

"My family? Why? What do you want to know?" She straightened away from him and he swore silently. He'd forgotten her reticence the other day.

Still, he cleared his throat, stubbornness taking hold of him. "You know a little about mine. You know I lost a sister when she was fairly young. It's only fair that I get to know a little about your family."

She closed her eyes and lowered her head a moment before again meeting his gaze. "I'm sorry. You're right. It's just…" She heaved a sigh. "My family…they're…different. I—" She shook her head. "I felt like I was being dragged into—I don't know—this circus or something and all I wanted was to live a peaceful, *normal* life."

"So your family's different. Isn't everyone's?"

"Not like mine." Her eyes widened. "But believe me, I am nothing like them. Not one bit. Maybe I was switched in the hospital, but I swear, I don't fit in." Her frustration seemed to reach out and grab him. "Have you ever felt that way?"

"No. I can't say that I have." He'd always fit so well with his family. An integral part. That was the problem.

Guilt filled him. He'd sought her out for her gift—for her healing heritage, and she wanted no part of it. The irony hit him so hard he stood staring at her, speechless.

She didn't seem to notice. "And they don't get it at all. They think I'm just like them. Which is such a crock, because I have *never* been like them."

"Would you like a drink?"

She sniffed. "Well, I don't normally drink while I'm working."

"I need a drink. Let's call this session officially over and you can toss the salad while I make the gravy and we can open a bottle of wine. I think we could both use a glass. What do you say?"

She pursed her lips and nodded. "Okay, maybe just this once."

"Great."

She followed him to the kitchen and laid her notebook on the counter while he opened a bottle of wine. After pouring two full glasses, he handed her one, then raised his in a toast. "To working together."

"Yes, to our new partnership."

"Partnership?"

"Oh, yes, I think of each new client as a partner. You'll be in on the decision-making process every step of the way."

He took a thoughtful sip. "Don't you ever have a client who just says, 'do whatever'?"

"Not usually, but there have been a few."

"And are they still partners?"

"I've usually found that people may not know what they want, but they always know what they don't want when they see it. The ones who say 'whatever' have never really meant it."

He pulled out a pan and a packet of gravy mix. As he stirred in a cup of water, he glanced at her. "I honestly don't care what you do with this place, though. I'm sure if you like it, I'll be happy with it."

"I'll still want you to look over samples and things. It's my policy to have you sign off on orders before they're placed. We don't want to make any expensive mistakes here. It's your dollar. I can work via e-mail some and I'll work around whatever schedule you'd like if you're concerned about me taking up too much of your time."

"E-mail is fine. I like the idea of a regular meeting schedule. I'll make myself available for you. I work out of my house at times, but I'm gone a good bit. I'll give you a key so you can come and go as you need." He handed her a cutting board, a knife and a cucumber. "Would you mind cutting this up?"

"I thought you said I'd be tossing the salad." She gestured at the bowl of lettuce he set beside her, a wry smile curving her lips. "This is not tossing the salad."

"Okay, would you please help me make the salad? Here, I'll slice the tomato."

"Go stir your gravy. I can do the tomato, too. I'm a girl of many talents."

He sipped his wine and let his gaze again drift over her. "No doubt."

She lowered her eyes as she sipped her wine. God, she was pretty. And sweet. And in total denial that she had the McClellan gift.

Turning back to the stove, he gave the gravy a hard stir. What kind of a jerk was he? He couldn't pursue a relationship with her—not just to benefit from any healing abilities she had. She'd hate him if she knew that was his original plan.

Well, the hell with that plan. It obviously wasn't going to work. Maybe Amanda could help him find some other voodoo healer or something. He could never ask Erin to do something she seemed so determined to avoid.

"You okay?"

He glanced at her, frowning. "Sure. Why?"

"You were rubbing your chest."

Shit. "Must have strained a muscle or something." He shrugged. "It's nothing."

Erin set down her knife. Jack was in some kind of discomfort. Besides the fact that he'd been rubbing his chest, she had this...feeling.

Her heart sped. The same jumble of emotions that had filled her in her shop swept over her, though this time it seemed calmer yet no less intense. Was this what Nikki and Tess felt? Was this the empathic nature they'd talked about? Why had she never felt this before Jack?

She had to know more about it. She *had* to touch him. The need was too strong to resist. She moved beside him. "Here, let me."

"I'm fine," he insisted, but she soothed her hand over his chest and he closed his eyes and stilled.

She shouldn't do this. She'd sworn off men, but for the life of her she couldn't remember why. It didn't matter, she couldn't have pulled away then had she wanted to. Moving her hands in small circles, she worked her way along his torso, her pulse thudding as she traced over his firm muscles. Desire flowed through her and she swallowed as he rolled back his head and a small moan of pleasure sounded from his throat.

It wasn't enough. She had to touch him—touch his skin. She had to know what this…connection was.

"Here, let me…." With quick twists of her fingers, she undid the buttons down the front of his shirt, then laid her hands on his warm skin, hardly believing she could be so bold.

His skin was tanned and smooth and so firm, she closed her eyes for a moment as pleasure rippled over her. He responded to her touch as no man had ever responded to her. She could feel his pleasure. It wrapped around her like a blanket and drew her in, bound her to him in some odd way she couldn't fathom at the moment, but when his gaze met hers, she stood breathless before him, his heart thrumming beneath her palms.

When his gaze fell to her mouth, she could feel him fighting the urge to kiss her. She struggled herself. In that moment there wasn't anything that made sense in the world but joining her mouth to his. He needed her. She knew that with a certainty that pushed her forward, made her press her lips to his, where she paused for just a heartbeat while their breath mixed, the warmth and excitement and anticipation almost unbearable.

So much for swearing off men.

Sighing, Erin parted her lips, and Jack's tongue met hers with little coaxing. He cupped her head and held her in place, and the hunger in him stirred a compassion in her that heated her blood. She kissed him back, her tongue stroking his, while she slipped her arms around his neck and pressed her body as close as she could get. Still it wasn't enough to satisfy his hunger—her hunger—the need he invoked in her.

He groaned and lifted her against him, his body hard, his hands cupping her bottom, kneading her, until she ground against him. Not wanting to break the kiss, craving the feel of his tongue, she held on and let the heat take her. For long moments the world revolved around that kiss—that endless joining of lips and tongues, their bodies straining against each other.

The timer on the oven blared. Slowly her senses untangled from his. His hands stilled on her, the heat of them branding her through her pants. Restraint punctuated his kiss, though his need hadn't abated. Somehow, for some reason, he was resisting whatever force had taken hold of them. He set her down, letting her body slide along his as the timer blared somewhere above the pounding of her pulse.

She stood mutely while he turned off first the timer and then the oven and stove. Then he took both her hands in his. "Erin, I shouldn't have done that."

She stared at him, the desire shining in his eyes. "You shouldn't have stopped?"

"No." He blew out a breath. "I shouldn't have kissed you like that."

"But I kissed you. I let it happen. I wanted it to happen."

"Erin—"

"You wanted it, too."

He nodded. "I did. Still, I shouldn't have."

"I don't know what to say. I've never done anything like that before. I just…" She just what? Couldn't help herself? Could barely keep herself from crawling all over him even now?

"You just what?" Something dark and painful swam in his eyes.

She cupped his cheek, unable to hold back the truth. "You needed me. I…couldn't help myself. I've never wanted anyone like that. You felt it, too."

"Yes, I did." The muscles in his jaw worked.

"But you stopped. Why?"

"It didn't… I don't want to push you into anything you're not completely comfortable with."

He tucked his hands into the back of his waistband, so his shirt spread wide, revealing the mouth-watering cut of his torso. Did he have any idea the picture he posed? Before she realized what she was doing, she pressed her palm over his heart.

He sucked in a breath and covered her hand with his. His gaze met hers, his desire raw and exposed. "Erin, I do need you."

Whether he pulled her into his arms or she moved there on her own, she couldn't say, but his mouth covered hers and his tongue stroked with a hunger and a need that eclipsed their earlier encounter. She sighed and let the fire take her. Whatever force brought them together, she was powerless to resist.

This time there would be no holding back.

Nothing could have prepared Jack for the power of Erin's kiss. Her tongue met his stroke for stroke, her hands seemed to touch him all over, arousing every nerve ending in his body. He burned for her. She was an enticing blend of innocence and vixen as she pulled his belt from its loops, then dropped it on the floor. When had she unbuckled it?

She broke the kiss only to run her mouth across his chest, kissing him over his heart so it pounded. Yet, for once, instead of pain, a strange euphoria filled him. Then her tongue darted over one of his nipples and he inhaled sharply as the pleasure coursed through him.

"Come." Her eyes sparkled as she tugged at his hand. "We never finished the tour. You didn't show me your bedroom."

Dazed, he followed her, his mind a fog of desire

and confusion. How had they gone from being non-dating partners to her dragging him to bed? All he knew was that she'd touched him and his knees had nearly buckled with his need for her.

Could that be it? Was it his need that triggered her gift, that turned her into the seductress?

She entered his room and he didn't have any more time to sort it out as she pushed him down onto his bed, then crawled on top of him. She kissed him and he lost himself to the heat of her mouth, the insistence of her tongue and the weight of her body as she moved against him, sending his blood pounding through his veins and hardening his cock.

His zipper grated and her fingers closed around him. He groaned as she stroked his aching hardness, but when she started to move down his body, he stopped her, needing to see her, needing to touch her everywhere before he gave himself to her.

She gasped as he tossed her to her back, her eyes wide, her cheeks flushed. What a siren she was as she helped him divest her of her blouse, then her pants. Her hands fumbled over his in her haste to remove her bra and panties. In moments she lay naked before him, her skin soft and smooth, her body petite but exquisite with her small waist flaring into the gentle swells of her hips. Her rosy nipples stood erect and inviting.

"Erin," he whispered, then ran his hand over her shoulder, down her arm to her hip. "You're so perfect. So beautiful."

She moved against the bed. "Touch me, Jack."

Her scent drifted over him and he buried his face between her breasts, surprisingly ample despite her small frame. He cupped her, kneading her until she moaned softly and arched up to him, silently begging him to take her into his mouth. He savored the feel of her nipple against his tongue as he suckled her long and hard while rolling the twin between his thumb and forefinger.

"Oh, sweet Jack." She parted her legs in invitation and he breathed deeply of her musky scent as he smoothed his hand down her belly, over her tangle of curls to the soft folds of her femininity.

She sighed softly as he dipped two fingers into her tight passage. She was hot and wet and his cock stirred with the need to plunge deep inside her. Still, the desire to pleasure her—to touch her and taste her—rose in him and he moved down her body, kissing a trail over that same path.

Shifting, she tilted her hips to give him better access as he scooped his hands beneath her buttocks and lifted her. He lowered his mouth to her. She shuddered as he licked along her folds, then dipped his tongue into her.

The taste of her.

"Jack, oh, Jack, that feels so good."

He ran his tongue along her clit and centered there, drawing circles around her with the tip of his tongue. She moaned and moved beneath him while he laved her.

"Oh, Jack…yes…yes."

Her sexy cries sent heat spiraling through him as he worked her swollen flesh, her pleasure somehow reaching out to him and filling him, burning through him. Her movements became more frantic and he gave her all she asked as she gripped his shoulders and moved against him.

"That's right, that's it…oh, yes…oh, yes…ah… ah…aah." Her body trembled and she cried out as her orgasm took her. She shuddered and moaned, and liquid heat pooled from her.

He drank his fill, her taste, her scent so right he couldn't get enough. At last she stilled and he moved back up her body, kissing her navel, her breast, where he lingered a while, until she moaned and he thought of that hot, sweet mouth of hers.

She slid her hands over him as he pulled back to look at her lying sated in his bed while he burned for her. Her gaze met his, and to his surprise, dark desire swam in her green depths. She wasn't sated. She wanted him still.

He kissed her then and again the kiss drew him in, spun him around, until all thought left his head, just the hunger and the sensations of her touching him, loving him with her mouth, with her hands and with her luscious body as she rubbed against him.

"Wait." He pushed back, then fumbled a condom from the nightstand drawer.

When he was ready, she pulled him on top of her and kissed him again. Her fingers slipped down his front to close again around him and he groaned into her mouth. She shifted, her tongue stilling as she nestled his cock against her clit. The pleasure was almost unbearable as he moved his hips, then slipped inside her. She was wet and hot and tight and she seemed to sense exactly what he needed as he thrust and she moved with him.

The heat, the pleasure spun around him in a tightening coil. He broke the kiss to nestle his head in the crook of her neck. Once more he thrust. Again. Then again, falling into a rhythm of give-and-take between them. Time seemed to stretch, then collapse. His breath came in short pants and he let the desire claim him as he sheathed himself over and over again in her heat.

Shudders racked him and he plunged deeper, faster. She moaned and trembled beneath him. She gripped his hips as her muscles contracted around him. She came with a force that sent him hurtling over the edge with her. He cried out as he emptied himself deep inside her.

For long moments he lay dazed beside her, his arm and one leg thrown across her. His heart thrummed in his ears and a feeling of euphoria filled him. He floated for a while, then she slid her hand along his chest, stopping over his heart.

Warmth suffused him. He brought her hand to his lips and kissed her palm, then she was in his arms again, her mouth soft and caressing on his. She pressed her body closer to him and, miracle of miracles, his cock stirred. "I still want you, Jack. That has to mean something, doesn't it?"

Rolling to his back, he carried her with him so that she straddled him. "It means I'm the luckiest man alive." He glanced down to where she rubbed herself along his hardening length. "Woman, you keep that up and I'll have you on your back again."

Her eyes shone as she settled more firmly against him. "Well, I hope you're a man of your word then."

6

ERIN CLOSED HER EYES AS the heat surged through her once more. How was she to resist when it felt so good, so right? Her clit burned as she ground against him. Every cell in her being hummed with excitement.

"Hold on." He tugged his pants up, then padded to the bathroom. When he returned, he was gloriously naked.

She let her gaze drift over him as he slipped on a new condom. "Hurry," she urged.

He cupped her breasts as he stretched out beside her. She settled over him again. He tilted his hips and thrust into her while he squeezed her nipples.

"Oh, Jack."

As before, he responded to her every movement. Her cries of pleasure sent desire spinning out from him and she gasped as he withdrew, then thrust up into her. She let the rhythm find her, the pleasure building deep inside her with each surge of her hips.

Her sex throbbed with delicious sensation, and the

heat took her in waves. He pulled her forward to take her nipple, and the feel of his hot mouth on her, suckling her, while she rode him was almost too much.

She pressed her palms to the headboard. "Jack…Jack…that feels…so good."

Taking his time, he savored first one breast, then the other, circling her nipple with his tongue while kneading her. She groaned as flames of desire licked through her. With his mouth and his cock both pleasuring her, she rode him faster, longer, harder.

Each pull of his mouth triggered a response deep inside her. Her blood heated and the wetness spilled from her as she moaned and increased her pace.

His tongue stilled and he groaned as she flexed her inner muscles in an intimate caress. Then he tugged hard with his mouth, and the first tremors of her release rippled outward. She opened her mouth in a wordless cry as she came, her climax hitting her in waves as she shuddered and stiffened over him.

He gripped her hips and thrust into her, straining toward his own orgasm. She tightened her muscles as the aftershocks of her climax flickered through her, and he found his release.

She wrapped her legs around him and rolled to her side, taking him with her and keeping her body joined with his. A state of peace descended over her. Never had she felt more complete.

Jack pressed a kiss to her cheek. "I'll be right back."

She groaned in protest as he pulled away from her to head into the bathroom again. The man was at least clean. She should follow him, slip into the shower with him. Unless…

She stared at the ceiling. What if he hadn't gone in there to clean up? What if she'd made him ill?

Sitting up, she clutched the sheet to her and strained to hear any sound from the bathroom. A hysterical laugh choked its way out of her as the significance of her actions dawned.

What in heaven's name had come over her?

The possibility that she might have made him ill sent panic through her. How could she have forgotten?

Jack emerged from the bathroom, a towel wrapped around his waist, a washcloth in his hand. His eyes sparkled as he slipped into the bed. "Why don't you relax and let me clean you?"

She scooted away from him. "I'm so sorry. I've never been so… If you want to hire another designer, I can make a few recommendations."

"Erin." He took her hand. "You don't want to quit because of this?"

"I don't know. Maybe I should. I've never behaved so unprofessionally. I'm not sure what came over me. It's shocking, really."

He rubbed circles around her knuckles with his

thumb. "Look, we didn't plan this. It just happened. There's obviously something between us. I don't know about you, but I thought what we just shared was pretty incredible. Is there any reason why we can't continue to work together and at the same time explore this attraction?"

The hope in his eyes was almost more than she could resist, but she had to. The energy between them was definitely different—much more intense than with any of her previous lovers. Would her effect on him be stronger? The last thing she wanted was to make him sick.

"I know this is going to sound bizarre after that little episode," she said, "but I've decided to give dating a rest."

He stilled. "Oh."

"It isn't you. Really. That was probably the most incredible sex I've ever experienced." Why did she feel compelled to speak so honestly with him? "It's me. I promise that when I say we shouldn't pursue any kind of a relationship, I'm thinking only of your best interest."

Disappointment swirled out from him and she held her breath.

"What if I don't agree that it's in my best interest for us to not see each other?" he asked.

"You have to trust me that it is."

Could it be that her gift was different in that it worked only with certain men—or with one man? And was it possible that such a man wouldn't be adversely affected by her gift?

She'd had sex—great, fantastic sex with a client. What kind of an idiot was she? She didn't deserve to have sex that good. "I'm sorry, I have to go."

"Wait."

She kicked aside the bedding, but her legs became tangled in the sheet and she groaned in frustration. "Damn it."

"Hold on." Jack stilled her, then untangled her with gentle movements. "We need to talk about this. Don't go off half-cocked."

"Half-cocked? No, that wasn't half-cocked. I would say that was pretty much fully cocked, whichever way you look at it."

"Erin, we're partners, in more ways than one, now. Let's talk this through."

She took a shuddering breath. "You're telling me that you still want me to do your interior decorating for you?"

"Yes. Absolutely."

"Even after…" She gestured toward the rumpled bed around them.

"We signed a contract."

"I won't hold you liable, Jack. I was grossly neg-

ligent and I will completely understand if you want
to tear up the contract."

"No way." He cupped her cheek and damn if his
mere touch didn't have her melting toward him. "I
was here, too. I hate that you would categorize what's
just happened between us as negligent. It was wild
and beautiful and…I can't describe it and do it jus-
tice, but something incredible is happening here."

Warmth and tenderness filled his gaze. The room
blurred and she blinked. Great, all she needed was to
go hormonal. He reached for her, the desire bright in
his eyes.

She pulled away and searched for her clothes. "I
have to go."

"Wait, Erin, we don't have to end the night like this."

"If I don't leave, we're just going to end up…"
She rolled her hand, indicating the bed.

"We don't have to. We could…talk."

"Right." He stood and her gaze slid over his bare
chest. Her pulse raced.

She scrambled from the bed, her clothes in hand,
and ran for the bathroom. What the hell was wrong
with her? This was so not normal.

JACK CLOSED HIS EYES and took a deep breath, but still
the room spun and his stomach churned. The pain in
his abdomen increased and he gripped his belly and

moaned. At least Erin had left before he'd embarrassed himself and gotten sick.

Erin. His mind drifted back over the past twenty-four hours. Had he really just met her yesterday? It hardly seemed possible.

His gut lurched. Bile burned his throat, and he stumbled to the bathroom, making it just in time to empty his stomach into the toilet. He heaved until he had nothing left, and still the spasms wracked him. Shaken and spent, he splashed water over his face, then rinsed his mouth.

Hell, he'd either eaten something that didn't agree with him or he'd picked up a stomach bug from somewhere. Hopefully he hadn't gotten Erin sick, too. It was bad enough he'd sent her running from his bed.

How had he let things get so out of control between them? If he'd had to sleep with her, why couldn't he have romanced her a little first? Memories of the almost wild way he'd taken her rolled over him.

No wonder she'd bolted.

Yet it seemed he lost his head when she touched him. Whatever healing power she had, Erin possessed some strong magic. He'd have to be better prepared when he saw her again—figure out a way to keep more focused.

The queasiness hit him again and he leaned

against the wall. A bead of sweat rolled down his cheek. He should call her—make sure she was okay. See if she was speaking to him.

After the way she'd left, chances were she wouldn't take his calls. Surely once she calmed down she'd remember how incredible it had been between them.

He splashed more cold water on his face, then staggered back to bed, where he collapsed. Rest. He just needed to rest.

His phone rang, but he didn't move to answer it. His answering machine kicked on and Bobby's voice sounded over the speaker. "Hey, bro, you there? I need some advice on some investments. What do you think about OTC stocks? Anyway, call me."

Jack shook his head. He'd call Bobby later. Guilt weighed on him, but Jack would figure out what to do about his family later. He couldn't think about that now. He had a more pressing matter at hand.

What to do about Erin?

One thing was for sure—no matter what else, he and Erin were meant to be together. Even she wouldn't be able to deny that. They simply needed to take things slowly. Tomorrow he'd call her and ask her out on a proper date. They'd figure the rest out then.

ERIN GRIPPED HER CAR keys on her way out late the next day. At the last moment, she turned to the living room of her new apartment. A sense of satisfaction filled her.

Boxes still filled the hallway and were scattered around the rest of the rooms, but she'd managed to unpack most of the living room. Every cushion, pillow and magazine was in place. No dirty gym socks lay strewn across the floor. No extra men mooned about or cluttered up the kitchen and bathroom. The coffee table remained clear of teacups filled with Aunt Sophie's special brews and books on the art of sexual healing. Peace and quiet and order reigned.

This was the normal she'd longed for.

Her world had not been irrevocably altered by her encounter with Jack Langston. She closed her eyes to savor the moment, but memories of last night drifted unbidden over her. Heat filled her cheeks.

At least he hadn't hurled in front of her. She would have been devastated had that been the case. In spite of her humiliation over her total loss of self-control, the fact that he'd remained healthy while she was with him lifted her spirits. Things could have gone worse.

She settled her purse strap over her shoulder. She should count her blessings. She had her new apartment. Her new *normal* apartment. Her new normal design business was holding its own. And she'd possibly slept with a man without making him ill.

Okay, maybe that wasn't all that normal—at least,

not for her, but it was certainly normal for regular people. That had to count for something. She tamped down on the thought that she'd left before he'd had much of a chance to get sick. All she knew was that since she'd branched out away from her wacky family into her nice new *normal* world, she'd felt tons better about her life.

So she'd completely lost her head over a man who happened to be a client and she'd slept with him without any concern for his health. She'd work on that.

She did need to talk to Jack and clear the air, though, and she should do it soon. Surely he would understand that they'd made a huge mistake in sleeping together. She couldn't pursue a relationship with him, not while he was a client.

She bolted the door behind her. As she headed to her car, a hawk circled overhead and a breeze ruffled her hair. What if Jack *was* different? He'd seemed fine last night. What if he were immune to her? She'd call him later to set up a civilized meeting with him where they could map out her strategy for the redesign of his condo. If she focused her efforts, she might be able to finish this project in a matter of weeks.

Smiling, she turned the ignition in her car. Then maybe they could pick up where they'd left off exploring this…thing between them. Her cell phone rang as she cruised along a street lined with tall palm trees and pastel-colored homes. She pulled the phone from her pocket, squinting against the afternoon sun. "Erin McClellan."

"Erin, it's Jack."

Her pulse kicked up a notch. "Hello, Jack. I was just thinking about you."

"Well, that's nice to know. I hope they were good thoughts."

Her face warmed as memories of his hands kneading her breasts, his mouth pleasuring her in the most intimate kiss, his body joined with hers, invoking exquisite sensations, rushed over her. The heat that had gripped her during their lovemaking flooded her. "Yeah, I guess you could say they were good thoughts."

"I've been thinking about you, too." His voice flowed like warm honey.

"Really? That's nice to know. Jack, we need to get together—talk this out."

"Exactly what I was thinking. What are you doing tonight?"

"I'm open after six."

"Why don't I take you out for a nice dinner?"

"Dinner?" Her heart sped. She'd meant to schedule a meeting with him, but this sounded suspiciously like a date.

His throaty laugh sounded across the line, sending gooseflesh rippling up her arms. "I figured if we were actually going to talk, we should do it in a nice public place."

"Okay…I guess public would be all right. It's…safe."

"Great. I'll pick you up at seven."

7

ERIN GLANCED AT HER clock, her stomach jumping. Jack would be here at any moment. She turned to her reflection in the mirror.

Her hair hung loose around her shoulders, and though she'd gone through half her closet and her dresser, she hadn't been able to find just the right outfit—the one that said she was a professional and not there to play around but that didn't totally disregard the fact that she was a woman, should he want to take note for future reference. Her gaze swept over the clingy slip she wore. If he showed up to find her in this, they'd never make it out the door.

Her phone rang and she jumped, her heart racing. It rang three more times while she dug through the pile of discarded clothes on her bed before she found the receiver, then another ring before she fumbled the thing to her ear. "Hello?"

"Hi." Jack's cool baritone sent butterflies scurrying inside her.

She clasped a handful of clothes to her chest. "Jack, hi."

"I think I've made a wrong turn."

"Where are you?"

He gave her a location just blocks away. He was practically at her door. She gave him directions. "But no hurry. Just take your time. I'm not ready yet."

She hung up and tossed the phone aside as she dashed to the closet. What was she going to wear?

A beige suit hung toward the back. She grabbed it and threw it on, tugging the hem of the skirt down as far as it would go. The thing still seemed shorter than she remembered. She ran to the mirror and gasped at the expanse of leg the skirt exposed.

Tess.

Her sister had borrowed the outfit last month and damn if she hadn't had the length altered. This would never do. With her heart thudding, Erin wriggled out of the skirt and top, then dug again into the closet. She pulled out a green dress she'd bought years ago. The fabric was soft but of good quality, and the cut classic, though the neckline scooped a little lower than she thought wise.

The ringing of her doorbell sounded and she tossed the dress over her head, then struggled to pull it down over her body without destroying her hair. Had it been this clingy the last time she'd worn it?

The fabric conformed to her breasts, then skimmed down over her stomach to flare gently at her hips.

She grabbed her shoes before stopping again in front of the mirror to stare at her refection in alarm. Pink colored her cheeks and the green of the dress brought out the green of her eyes. She combed her fingers through her hair but couldn't tame the wild look of it.

And the dress… Well, he'd certainly realize she was all woman. The bell rang again and she grabbed her purse. No time to change. It would be up to her to convey the professional attitude she needed for this discussion with Jack.

"YOU LOOK BEAUTIFUL tonight." Jack shoved his hands into his pockets to keep from touching Erin. They walked along the tropical garden outside the restaurant where they'd just eaten.

He wanted to take time to get to know her better and let her get to know him, but the woman looked so good it was all he could do to keep from jumping her. Had he been so remiss in his love life lately that all he could think about was how it had felt to hold her and bury himself deep inside her?

Her cheeks colored, a sight that sent his pulse speeding as memories of her, flushed and panting, in his bed flowed over him. She smoothed her hand over her hair. "I feel a little thrown together."

"It's a good look for you."

"Thank you," she said. "You look nice, too."

She had refused his offer of wine earlier, so he had abstained also. He hadn't wanted to push the romantic angle. They'd have time for that later. It was enough that she had let him take her out tonight.

He smiled at how her eyes had widened at the portions when their meal was served. She had dug into her roasted chicken, her face lit with pure pleasure. She was a sight as she savored each bite.

"Erin, thank you for agreeing to go out with me tonight. I know you were reluctant, but it was important to me that we have an official date."

She stopped, her eyebrows raised. Then she carefully started walking again. "That's what I want to talk to you about."

He moved closer to her and couldn't resist taking her hand. Warmth shot through him. "I understand this is all happening rather unexpectedly, but that doesn't make it wrong."

Her gaze softened and, to his relief, she kept her hand nestled in his. "I'm not denying there's chemistry between us, Jack."

"Good, because I want to explore this chemistry. Don't you?"

She hesitated a long moment. "Yes, I do, but the timing is wrong. You see that, don't you?"

"No."

"It's a conflict of interest."

"How? I want you. You want me. Sounds like we're both interested in the same thing."

"You want me now. I want you later—after I finish the redesign of your home."

He traced circles over the inside of her wrist with his thumb. Her pulse throbbed steady and strong beneath his touch. "You want me now."

With a groan, she slid her hand from his. "It doesn't matter. I have a serious work ethic. Metro Miami may be a fairly big place, but the design community is a close-knit group. The networking that goes on there can make or break a career. I've been on the fringes for a long time and recently I seem to be making some headway. I can't be seen as anything but professional with this group if I want to get somewhere."

He crossed his arms. "And this group, they're people your family would approve of?"

"My family? What do they have to do with it?"

"Family is everything."

She glanced away. "My family is an open-minded bunch. It isn't usually a question of them accepting other people. It's more whether other people will accept them."

"So tell me about them. What about them might make them hard to accept?"

"My mother and sisters are all quite beautiful. You'd be as enamored of them as any male. It's the rest of the population that tends to take issue."

"You mean the female population?"

She shrugged. "What does it matter?"

"It matters because they're who you are, where you come from. I can't imagine what my life would be like without my family." Or what theirs would be like without him.

"I'm sure you have a nice, normal family."

He shook his head. Too many of his relatives tended to live short, sweet lives. How normal was that? "I don't know that there's any such thing. Mine comes as close as any I suppose. We still have our issues, as everyone does. You just deal with them."

"Well, I'm dealing with mine."

"How?"

She stared at him, unblinking, for a long moment. "I've made a conscious choice to build my own life."

"Away from your family?"

"More or less. Both of my sisters had moved out of the apartment we used to share and the lease was up. I didn't need such a big place all to myself. It made sense to move."

"So how far away did you move?"

"What does that matter?"

"You've run away."

Her eyes narrowed. "What is wrong with wanting to walk my own path? I see them. I talk to them. In fact, I'm having lunch with my sister and my mother tomorrow afternoon. We're planning my oldest sister's bridal shower."

"That's great. I'm happy to hear that." He pursed his lips. Though he preferred not to discuss his own family, he couldn't resist the urge to get her to talk some more about hers. "Tell me about them—your mother and sisters and anyone else."

"I'm not sure what you want to hear," she said. "My oldest sister, Nikki, is a veterinarian. She has her own practice. My other sister, Tess, owns a nursery. And my mother…well, she's an artist, though she…may be retiring soon. She's spent a lot of her time traveling all over the world."

"They don't sound so unusual." Except that she'd failed to mention their not-so-normal sexual-healing capabilities. Did that mean that was at the root of her discontent?

"I guess they're not." She shook her head. "Except… Well, they have some unusual beliefs. They're into the whole metaphysical scene."

He straightened. "And you're not?"

"I fail to see what all this new-age-woo-woo fuss is about."

He should tell her. He should admit right now that

he'd heard all about the McClellan women and their magic touch. "Erin, I—"

"I mean, they actually believe they heal men by sleeping with them. Can you imagine that? How nuts can you get?" She raised her hands in surrender. "There you have it. The dark secret of my family. They're crazy. Stark raving lunatics."

"Why do you say that? I've been looking into the metaphysical scene and I find a lot of it quite interesting."

Her shoulders heaved and she looked suddenly tired. "To each his own. I just don't need to be around all that craziness. I need a more…normal grounded-in-reality kind of life. I'm tired of people looking at me askance because I'm one of *them.* I could never…do what they do—that whole sexual-healing thing. That isn't what I want in a relationship."

Guilt filled him. "There are worse things to build a relationship on."

Her gaze narrowed. "Do you know that men still seek out my sister, Tess? She's settled with Mason. They seem to be living that elusive happily ever after. She's not looking for a new relationship, yet men still seem to come out of the woodwork to woo her. Maybe not as many as before, but she still gets the occasional guy."

She shuddered. "It's creepy. They hear about her

from a friend of a friend—Tess has more *friends* than you can shake a stick at—then they approach her all hopeful and expectant. I think I would truly lose it if that happened to me. Thank God nobody knows me. I'm the younger sister, the forgotten one. Believe me, in my family I'm a bit of an aberration, like the redheaded stepchild, only I'm the blonde.

"I get that from my father, whom I've seen pictures of but have never met. We each have different fathers, you know—my sisters and me. Maggie, our mother, never stayed with one lover for more than a few months at a time. Somewhere along the way she decided to have the three of us, or so she insists. I'm thinking at least one of us had to be an accident, possibly all three, though she would never admit it—just moved us along from lover to lover, house to house. Nikki hated it every bit as much as I did, but Tess is so much like her—"

She stopped, her eyes round. "I'm so sorry. I don't know where all that came from. I tend to talk when I get nervous."

"No problem."

"The point is that I am nothing like them, especially Tess and Maggie. Nikki wasn't so crazy about the "gift" until she met Dylan and now she's fine with it—with him. Me…" She took a deep breath. "I just can't condone the whole sexual-healing thing. If ever a man came to me wanting me to sleep with him and heal him, I guess I'd have to laugh. The whole thing is really crazy. Don't you think so, Jack?"

He stared at her for one speechless moment. How the hell was he supposed to answer that?

"You were okay last night, weren't you? I mean after we…you know?" Her gaze pierced his, seeking, searching for whatever truth he might hide.

Why would she ask that? Should he tell her he'd been ill? It didn't seem to matter. He'd woken up this morning with more energy than he'd had in months. Judging by the way she'd attacked her food, she hadn't suffered any ill effects.

"Jack? You okay?"

"Fine. I woke up today feeling like I could conquer the world. Haven't felt that good in I don't know how long."

"Really?" Her gaze darkened in that way that melted his insides. "That's wonderful. I'm so happy to hear that. I slept like a rock myself."

He tamped down on the little voice that whispered he was lying by omission. His illness last night didn't have anything to do with Erin. Besides, what if it had something to do with his heart? He'd have to check with his doctor, but for now he wasn't ready to tell her about his condition.

A cool breeze brushed over them. He faced her. "You seemed upset when you left."

"That wasn't like me at all last night. I can't imagine what you must think of me. I swear that I have never come on to anyone like that, especially not a client."

"You're the best thing that's happened to me in a very long time. I want you to do my condo, but if the whole client thing is an issue, then we can always delay this job. Or I can find someone else."

"That's entirely up to you. I won't hold you to that contract and I'll return your deposit if that's what you want."

"No, that isn't what I want. But I want you to be comfortable working with me and…" He took her hand again. "I want to be with you."

"Jack—"

"We'll be discreet. I don't know anyone in the design circles except for you. I want to get to know you, Erin. I want more nights like last night and I don't see why we have to wait until you're finished with the redesign on my house.

"That's much less important. If you can tell me that's what you truly want, then I'll do my best to leave you alone, but you have to tell me honestly that you don't want me. Can you do that?" he asked.

Her gaze again met his and a sense of well-being settled over him. A small smile played across her lips. "No, Jack, I can't."

His smile matched hers and his body hummed with anticipation. "So does that mean I get a good-night kiss when I take you home tonight?"

The curve of her throat captured his gaze. He imagined kissing her there, his mouth watering for the taste of her.

She stopped and turned to him. "Why don't you take me home and find out?"

8

HEAT COURSED THROUGH Erin as Jack pressed her to the wall and kissed her neck. How they'd made it back to her apartment was a blur. One minute they'd been walking after sharing a civilized meal and the next they'd been falling through her door on top of each other.

She should stick to her guns, revive her plan to give up men. But Jack wasn't just any man, and all her well-thought-out intentions flew out the window when he was near.

His mouth skimmed over her collarbone, then up her neck, sending awareness shimmering through her. Hell, she'd known in the restaurant she wouldn't be able to protest. He hadn't been ill last night. The thought sent happiness and desire flowing through her.

Had she found the one man she could be with?

She tugged his already unbuttoned shirt from his pants, then slid her hands up his abdomen, over his chest, her fingertips alive with the feel of warm, hard muscle beneath them.

"I want you, Erin," he said, his voice rough with desire.

She wrapped her arms around his neck and pressed her body so close to his, his heart thudded against her breast. His mouth found hers and his tongue greeted her with hungry strokes. For long moments she stood mesmerized by his kiss, her body drinking in the feel of him so near, his scent wrapped around her and his hands stroking her, holding her close.

Then he traced his mouth down her throat to the neckline of her dress, where he kissed the slight swell of each breast visible there while he caressed her through her clothes. She closed her eyes and pressed her hands to the wall behind her.

He drew back, his eyes dark as he slipped his hand under her dress, pushing the hem up her thigh. "You're so beautiful."

She reached for him, tugging him close for another kiss as he cupped her bottom, cradling her in his palm. She kissed him long and hard and deep, savoring the feel of his tongue, his teeth, his lips on her while he continued to touch her, his fingers tracing along her thigh to the edge of her panties, then beyond, until he stroked the folds of her femininity, coaxing the wetness from her. Her heart thrummed in her ears and her sex pulsed.

Moaning, she shifted and he slipped two fingers

deep inside her. He stroked her with a restraint he hadn't had before, and she moved against him, silently pleading with him to not hold back. He broke the kiss to whisper in her ear. "Baby, come for me. I'll give you whatever you want, just let me love you."

"Yes, Jack." She gripped his arms as he thrust his fingers repeatedly into her.

Heat coiled through her, and her clit throbbed as she moved her hips in sync. "Oh…Jack."

"You feel so good." With his free hand he reached up under her dress to cup her breast. He kneaded her, then tugged aside her bra. With every thrust of his fingers, he circled her nipple with his thumb, working it into a hard point.

Sounds of pleasure tore from her as the heat swallowed her. Then his mouth was on her throat and the first ripples of orgasm washed over her. Gasping, she strained against him, then gripped his shoulders and let the sensations take her. She came in one long wave.

He withdrew his fingers to spread her wetness over her clit, working her tender flesh until she writhed against him. The tension coiled through her. He took his time, fondling her with devoted attention to her every gasp and whimper. When she caught her rhythm again and ground into him, he took her cue, increasing his efforts. She came again, the pleasure so intense she cried out with it.

He dropped to his knees before her, stripped off her panties, then shoved her dress up. He draped her leg across his shoulder, then laved her with gentle strokes of his tongue.

She inhaled a sharp breath and tried to move away from him, the sensations too intense. "Oh, no…wait."

But he held her fast and licked along her folds before delving his tongue into her heat. When she moaned, he withdrew to circle her clit. The fire again burned through her. She pressed her hands to the wall once more as the tension reached an almost unbearable level. Gasping with need, she rocked against him as she climaxed for a third time.

He moved up her body and she welcomed his lips on her as he kissed her with hungry desperation. His desire coursed strong and wild through him, energizing her in a way she couldn't have been otherwise. She unzipped his pants, then slipped her hand around his hard cock. The pleasure flowing from him stole her breath as she stroked him, his heat and silky hardness an enticing mixture.

A boldness she'd never known gripped her and she pressed him to the wall and met his gaze. "It's my turn. I'm going to eat you up."

A stifled moan was her only answer as she pulled him free of his confining briefs and knelt before him. He buried his fingers in her hair as she went down on him, savoring the exquisite feel of him. Never had she enjoyed pleasuring a man like this.

His excitement caught her up and held her captivated as she explored every delectable inch of him. When she took him into her mouth, his pleasure was so intense it shot through her to her own sex, making her wet and swollen and needy all over again. She loved him with her mouth and he moved against her, the sounds straining from him urging her on, increasing her desire.

"Erin…ah, sweet…oh, Erin." He moaned her name over and over as she savored the taste of him, his scent heavy in her nostrils.

Her own need grew with his. She rose and the heat in his eyes nearly consumed her. With one movement she pulled her dress over her head, then dropped it on the floor. He took her mouth, kissing her with a force that left her senseless or so full of sensation she couldn't tell the difference.

She pressed against him. And he pulled the straps of her slip over her arms until the silky garment floated into a puddle around her feet. She yanked off his shirt and he stepped out of his pants.

"Come with me," she said, smiling at her double meaning, and took his hand to pull him into her bedroom.

He hit the mattress beside her and they divested each other of their remaining clothes between kisses and strokes and sighs of pleasure. She pulled back to admire him as he lay naked before her, his torso sculpted, his stomach cut, his erection full and his gaze heavy with desire. He opened his arms and she went to him, kissing him again as the same sweet longing filled her.

Then he stilled and she pushed back to look at him. "Jack?"

"I wasn't thinking we'd end up doing this again. I meant to take things slow, give you a chance to get to know me."

"You don't want to do this?" She stared at him, frowning. Of course he wanted her. His urgency curled around her.

"I have never wanted anyone or anything the way I want you now."

"Good." She shifted so his cock rested against her clit. She moved sensuously. "I want you, too."

"Wait."

"It feels so good, Jack."

"Wait." He gripped her shoulders. "Do you have protection?"

She rolled off him. "Damn."

A sound of torment ripped from him. She reached over to pat him. "It's okay. Look in that box on the nightstand." She dropped her head into her hands. "I just can't believe I forgot."

"I nearly did, too." A rustling sounded as he dug in the box.

A moment later his warmth covered her back and his hands cupped her breasts. He pulled her against him and she closed her eyes as he teased her nipples into hard peaks. When she could wait no longer, she turned to him and pushed him down onto the pillows. "No more playing around. It's time we got serious here."

"No argument from me." His gaze darkened and his fingers found her swollen sex. He parted her and then he slipped inside her.

She sighed with relief as he filled and stretched her, his hardness stroking her clit as he moved inside her. Then she was on her back beneath him and he was thrusting with an abandon that had her moaning and holding on as the sensations swept through her, his pleasure and her own coiling through her.

Deep, then deeper he drove into her, and still she urged him on, encouraging him with her body and her words, until the heat claimed her and she lost herself to the collage of feelings sweeping over her. Her sex throbbed, her clit burned and a feeling of wonder filled her as again her climax took her and she cried out with the intensity of it, barely aware he continued to stroke into her. Then he gripped her close and shuddered. The power of his orgasm crashed over her until she lay stunned, with him collapsed on top of her.

She closed her eyes and floated. His heart beating so close to hers, it seemed they beat in sync. Suddenly he pushed away from her. "Which way to the bathroom?"

"There." She pointed, frowning as he swerved into the adjoining bathroom.

She stared up at the ceiling, unease filling her. *Please don't let him be getting ill.* She calmed her rising panic, forcing herself to take long breaths and count. For endless moments it seemed she lay there, losing track, then starting over again.

Twenty-four…twenty-five…twenty-six…

After a while she gave up and padded to the door. The shower splashed on and she hesitated. Did that mean he was all right? Still, he'd left so abruptly.

Something was wrong.

She turned to leave and the door opened. Jack stood in the opening, steam swirling around him. "Hi. I was just coming to get you."

His warmth and desire again reached out to her as he pulled her toward the pulsing water. "I was worried about you," she said. "You left so quickly. Is everything okay?"

Light shone in his eyes. He moved her under the warm spray. "Everything is absolutely fine." He wrapped his arms around her and nuzzled her ear. "What could I possibly complain about when I have you?"

His body pressed into hers and the steam and the heat enfolded them. She brushed aside her worries as his mouth took hers in a kiss that started them again on that journey to bliss.

For now, all that mattered was being with Jack.

CLASSICAL MUSIC SOUNDED from a hidden speaker as green-aproned servers skirted among the crowded tables. Erin sipped her iced tea and tamped down on her impatience. She'd hardly arrived and she couldn't wait for this lunch to be over.

She needed to get to Jack's.

Besides promising him she'd come by his condo with some of the design workups she'd put together for him, she had to figure out what was wrong between them. Not that the goodbye kiss he'd given her left any doubt that he'd been thrilled with their love-making and couldn't wait to have her back in his arms and in his bed.

She had a feeling that something was wrong. She'd questioned him again about his abrupt departure from bed, but he'd insisted he'd been fine. He'd certainly seemed more than fine when he'd made love to her for over an hour in the shower.

"What are you going to have?" Tess drew Erin's attention to the present. Tess glanced over the menu, her eyes sparkling. "They have a new salad. I think I'll have that."

"And?" Maggie looked questioningly at her, her eyelids slightly drooping.

Erin had been distressed to see the physical evidence of Maggie's decline, but she kept her expression light so as not to spoil their lunch.

"And sweet tea with lemon." Smiling, Tess set aside her menu.

"That's it?" Erin stared at her sister in disbelief as her own stomach growled.

"That's it." Tess's fingers tapped over the slick cover of the menu.

"Are you dieting?" Maggie asked.

"Don't feel like ordering more. Shall we start with the guest list?"

Maggie blinked, staring at her a moment, then she looked to Erin and shrugged. "Okay, but I'm starved. How about you, Erin?"

"I'm pretty hungry," Erin said. She'd been eating like a horse the past few days, but her stomach rumbled again and her mouth watered as she glanced over the assortment of entrées. "I'm not sure. I can't decide between the blackened snapper or the roast beef and garlic potatoes."

Maggie smiled. "Get them both. You can always take some home for later."

Both? She never double ordered off the menu. That was Tess's thing. Yet she couldn't seem to fill her belly lately. It seemed no matter what she ate she was hungry again in a few short hours. "Maybe I will order them both, so I can snack on one later."

"That's the spirit." Maggie patted her leg. "I'm with you." She turned to Tess. "Are you sure you're feeling okay, dear?"

"I'm feeling just fine," Tess said.

"But you're not eating."

"Yes I am. I'm eating salad."

"Since when is salad food? I'm going to have to speak with Mason about this. Is the man starving you?" Maggie frowned.

"Salad *is* food and this doesn't have anything to do with Mason. In fact, that man has learned how to order large in a big way. He doesn't always take to-go boxes either."

That seemed to satisfy Maggie to some extent. Their waitress arrived shortly and took their order. After she'd gone, Tess pulled out a pen and pad of paper. "Let's start with the guest list."

"Let's keep it small," Maggie said. "Nikki made me promise we wouldn't go overboard."

"Here's what I have so far." Tess turned the notebook toward their mother, who leaned over the page with her.

Erin folded her arms. It was nice that Tess had wanted to include her, but Tess and Maggie could pull this together without her help. From their long, wavy red hair to their fiery tempers the two were a matched pair.

As usual, Erin felt the odd man out.

Their food came and for a short while she lost herself in the fresh vegetables, spicy fish and tender beef. Her taste buds came alive with each bite. When had food tasted so good?

"Sweetie, do you want dessert?" Maggie asked. "You seem to have a healthy appetite today."

Erin's gaze swung from her nearly empty plate to her mother and her sister. A feeling of unease crept over her. "I just—"

"Who is he?" Tess asked.

"Don't press her." With a frown Maggie shooed Tess back.

A buzzing sounded in Erin's ears. "What do you mean? Who is who?"

"Who is *he?*" Tess asked again, her gaze dropping to the remains of both of Erin's entrées.

Erin frowned. How could she have eaten so much? Strange as it seemed, she wasn't bursting at the seams, though. She just felt…content. The hunger that had been gnawing at her for the last couple of days had at last abated.

"Tess, you know she doesn't like to talk about those things," Maggie scolded.

"I don't like to talk about what things?" Erin asked. "So I was hungry, and yes, I do think I'll order dessert." She flipped through the menu that stood on the table. "That chocolate-fudge brownie looks good. I think I'll try that."

"Ah, yes, chocolate always hits the spot for me." Maggie pulled the menu toward her, then frowned and handed it to Tess. "Will you please pick for me, sweetie?" She waved her hand in front of her face. "I, uh, forgot my glasses."

Erin's stomach tightened, but Tess didn't miss a beat. "I say three chocolate-fudge brownies. There, does that make you feel better?"

"Much," Maggie said with a grateful smile.

"There's the nursery calling," Tess said and pulled her cell phone from her purse, its musical ring clamoring over the myriad conversations around them. Frowning, she turned aside to speak to the caller.

Their server took their dessert orders. Tess bit her lip as she put away her phone. "I'm afraid I'm going to have to take mine to go."

"Oh, dear, is everything all right?" Maggie asked.

"Evan is going home sick. I have to get to the nursery. We have a big shipment coming in. I'm sorry to cut things short."

"It's okay, honey. You do what you have to. Maybe Erin can drive me home to save you some time."

Erin straightened. "Whatever you need."

"We can tie up a few of these shower details while we wait for those desserts." Maggie whipped out the notepad and they ran through a list of options with quick efficiency, so they had the shower planned by the time the brownies arrived.

"You two are the best." Tess rose, then hugged first her mother and then her sister. "I'd be dead meat without you."

"No you wouldn't, dear, but it's sweet of you to say so," Maggie said. "You tell Mason I want to see more of the both of you. Nothing would please me more than if we were planning a double wedding."

Tess's eyes rounded. "I'm not giving him any ideas. The man has already been mooning about tying me down and making an honest woman of me."

Maggie nearly jumped out of her seat. "Mason asked you to marry him? Why didn't you say so? Now you have to go without giving us all the details."

"We're as good as married now. And besides, we've already got our hands full with Nikki's wedding plans. Enough." She held up her hand when their mother would have said more. "I have to run. Poor Evan is miserable. We'll talk later."

She picked up her purse and turned to Erin. "Thanks for taking Mom home. You call me. We'll do another girls' night."

As she moved away, weaving a path between the tables, a feeling of desolation stole over Erin, but she shook it off. Why would she be upset over Tess and Mason possibly tying the knot? It shouldn't bother her any more than Nikki's impending nuptials.

And why would that upset her? She was happy for her sisters. Truly happy.

Besides, she had Jack waiting for her. It wasn't as if her life was devoid of joy or anything. So she hadn't inherited the McClellan gift. If Jack had been sick last night, he'd hid it well. His continued health gave her hope that she could have a normal relationship with a man. If that meant bending her rules of professionalism a bit, then so be it.

"You ready, hon?" Maggie's soft voice brought Erin out of her reverie.

"Sure." She gathered her purse. "Let's go."

Maggie took her arm and Erin guided her out of the restaurant. Her throat tightened as her mother leaned heavily on her arm. Maggie had always been so free-spirited and independent. Now her fingers dug into Erin's arm in a grip that conveyed that, in spite of her calm demeanor, Maggie was afraid.

The realization filled Erin with sorrow. Outside, Maggie barely blinked at the bright sunlight. Erin's concerns over Jack could wait. For once, her mother needed her. And Erin meant to be there for her.

9

TWENTY MINUTES LATER Maggie turned to Erin from the passenger seat, a knowing smile on her face. "So you have a new young man."

Surprise rippled through Erin. "There are no secrets in this family."

"No, not normally. You couldn't have kept it a secret if you had wanted to, sweetheart. If your voracious appetite wasn't a dead giveaway, then that light in your eyes would have done it. You have moments when you are positively glowing. Now why would you want to keep such a thing a secret?"

Erin turned in to her aunt Sophie's driveway. "There is someone. I'd just rather keep it private."

"Is everything okay?"

"Of course. Why would there be anything to worry about?" Surely whatever Jack was keeping from her couldn't be any worse than her not telling him she was Typhoid Mary.

"Are you sure? You seem…a little off."

"I'm just adjusting to my new place and revamping my business."

"I hear that's going well."

Erin braced herself for the same lecture she'd heard from both Nikki and Tess on her giving up feng shui. "It has been. Very well, in fact. I've just signed a new client."

"Oh, I see." Her mother's sideways glance sent apprehension skittering up her spine, though she made no comment about the feng shui.

"You see what?" Why had she thought that she could keep anything from Maggie? The woman was a walking lie detector.

Maggie's shoulders shifted in a slight shrug. "You have mixed emotions about this young man. Guilt. What are you feeling guilty about? Something to do with your work." Her eyebrows lifted. "He's a client."

Busted. "How is it that you always know these things?"

"Sweetie, you are so easy to read. One of the easiest. You have the ability, too."

"I don't think so. I'm not like you."

"I suppose that's true. We have never been much alike, and the gift manifests differently in each of us. Plus you and your sisters are a whole new generation. But you still have the gift, and part of that is the empathic nature," Maggie said. "You feel it with your young man. You feel what he feels. It bonds you in a way you can't escape."

"Maybe."

"Certainly it does." Maggie lifted her purse strap to her shoulder. "Do you want to come inside? Thomas has made some adjustments to my studio. Nothing like you would have done, hon, and I think we could do more with the lighting. It still isn't right. Maybe you could tell me your opinion?"

"I have some lights I got in the other day that aren't going to work for what I had in mind. Maybe we can do something with those."

"Great, sweetie, now call that young man and let him know I'll keep you just a few short minutes. I'll meet you inside."

"No, it's okay. It'll be fine. I'll get there when I get there."

"You sure?"

"Absolutely." Erin followed her mother up the walk.

Out of the blue, memories of classmates' teasing flowed over Erin. Maggie's constant shuffling from man to man hadn't escaped their notice. In spite of the agony, Erin had endured. She loved her mother and she meant to help her in any way possible.

As they ascended the stairs leading to the wide wraparound porch, Maggie missed a step, stumbling against Erin. She clutched the rail and grabbed

Maggie's arm to stabilize her. Her heart raced. "Are you okay?"

Maggie nodded, her mouth set in a firm line. "I'm sorry, dear, that was clumsy of me. I just…I didn't see the damn thing."

Erin took a deep breath. "It's okay."

"No. It isn't." Maggie stopped halfway up the stairs. "I've got the good sense not to drive myself around anymore, but there is no reason why I can't walk up a flight of stairs on my own."

"But, Maggie—"

"Don't 'but Maggie' me. I will not have everyone coddling me. This is exactly why I didn't want to tell all of you."

"Now wait a minute. I was not coddling you. You nearly fell. I caught you. Thank God we didn't both go tumbling down these stairs."

All the fight seemed to drain from her mother. She ran her hand across her eyes. "You're right. I'm sorry. It gets a little frustrating at times."

Erin's throat tightened. "Of course it does. It's perfectly understandable. But you have got to cut yourself some slack. You're going through an adjustment period." Her voice faltered and she stopped.

Maggie wrapped her arm around her. "It'll be okay, pumpkin. I'm not sure how, but somehow, some way, this is all going to work out just fine."

Not trusting her voice, Erin nodded and Maggie let her go to take the rest of the stairs on her own, her head held high. When they reached the top, she turned to Erin, smiling, though her drooping eyes appeared unfocused. "See? I merely have to concentrate on not being so clumsy. You certainly don't have to see stairs to climb them."

"No, I suppose not."

"I've started classes you know," Maggie said as they pushed through the front door.

"What kind of classes?"

All the familiar smells of Aunt Sophie's house wrapped around Erin, an assortment of herbs and spices and sunshine that made this the one place all the girls ran to when they needed comfort or just a friendly ear. No wonder Maggie had chosen to stay here. The rustling of pots sounded from the kitchen and Sophie emerged, her hair tied up in a bandanna.

"You brought us a special treat," she said as she kissed Erin's cheek. "Don't mind me, I'm in a cleaning mood."

"She's going to see what she thinks about the lighting," Maggie said.

Sophie blew out a long breath. "It's always about that damn lighting. If she's going to paint blindfolded, I don't see what the big deal is. What does it matter? It's a bunch of nonsense, is what I say. Don't you think so, Erin?"

"Tell me about your classes, Maggie. Are they some kind of art classes?" Erin asked, hoping to change the subject.

Of course, the notion of Maggie continuing her painting was absurd. She had to accept that her painting career was coming to an end. A shiver of sadness raked through Erin and she blinked back unwanted moisture from her eyes.

"Thank you, darling, for not agreeing with my sister—or for at least not saying so." Maggie moved into the sunroom. "I know I said we'd make it quick, but just sit with me for a minute. Sophie, you'll get us some tea, won't you? I haven't had my special blend yet today. I forgot it this morning."

"I'll get your tea. Meanwhile, maybe your sensible daughter will talk some sense into you," Sophie said, then moved off into the kitchen.

After she'd gone, Maggie sank to the soft cushions of a lounger and motioned Erin to the love seat near it. "She's fretting, you know. You can always tell because she gets in these cleaning moods and she scours everything. It's driving me crazy, but she's my sister. I love her. And she's been a dear to let me stay while I sort things out."

"So how are you? Really?"

Maggie didn't answer for a minute, just stared into space. "I have my good days and my bad days." She shrugged. "But what am I going to do? It is what it is. These classes are helpful. My doctor recommended them." She chuckled softly. "I wish they were art classes. They're classes for the visually impaired. They're teaching me how to cope with everyday things like stairs and fixing breakfast and setting up my environment."

"Maggie—Mom, how can I help?"

"You can not worry about me or feel sorry for me. Lord knows I've done enough of that myself and I am sick to death of it."

She swung her feet over the edge of the lounger. "Let's go look at the studio, then send you on your way. Who am I to hold you hostage with poor-me stories when you have a hottie waiting for you."

"It's okay. I haven't seen much of you lately."

"Come." Maggie rose, motioning to Erin as she headed to a room adjoining the sunroom.

One side of the studio faced the backyard. Floor-to-ceiling windows overlooked Aunt Sophie's herb garden. Birds flitted from the branches of trees at the center of the garden. "The natural lighting is good, like in the sunroom."

Erin flipped a switch on the wall. Soft light shone over a half-painted canvas and an assortment of brushes and paint stored in neat bins on a nearby worktable. "This is nice backlighting Thomas put in, but maybe we can try some halogens. I'll see if I can get Thomas to help me with them over the weekend."

"He'll be by tomorrow. Do you want me to ask him?" The hope in Maggie's eyes was more than Erin could resist.

"Have him call me when he gets ready to head this way and I'll see if I can meet him."

Maggie squeezed her hands. "Thank you, dear. Now are you or are you not going to tell me about this new crush of yours? I have never had such a dry spell, self-imposed or not. I am dying for a little romance. Just tell me how you met."

Her mother looked so young and full of life in that moment, Erin couldn't help but squeeze her hands in return and smile. "He walked right into my shop the other day."

"And did your heart do a little dance at the sight of him?"

"I guess it did."

"Oh, look at you glow. I can see that well enough." Maggie dropped her hands. "You run on to him. Tell him I'm sorry to have kept him waiting."

"He's supposed to be working."

"Right, well that's going to stop the minute you walk through his door, hon. Go, enjoy."

Get FREE BOOKS and a FREE GIFT when you play the...

LAS VEGAS

GAME

Just scratch off
the gold box with a coin.
Then check below to see
the gifts you get!

YES! I have scratched off the gold box. Please send me my **2 FREE BOOKS** and **gift for which I qualify.** I understand that I am under no obligation to purchase any books as explained on the back of this card.

351 HDL D7XN   151 HDL D7YP

FIRST NAME   LAST NAME

ADDRESS

APT.#   CITY

STATE/PROV.   ZIP/POSTAL CODE   (H-B-10/05)

7	7	7	Worth TWO FREE BOOKS plus a BONUS Mystery Gift!
🍒	🍒	🍒	Worth TWO FREE BOOKS!
🔔	🔔	♣	TRY AGAIN!

BUSINESS REPLY MAIL
FIRST-CLASS MAIL   PERMIT NO. 717-003   BUFFALO, NY

POSTAGE WILL BE PAID BY ADDRESSEE

HARLEQUIN READER SERVICE
3010 WALDEN AVE
PO BOX 1867
BUFFALO NY 14240-9952

NO POSTAGE
NECESSARY
IF MAILED
IN THE
UNITED STATES

"Here's the tea." Aunt Sophie set a tray on the table. "And you're leaving, aren't you?"

"She has a hot young thing waiting for her." Maggie winked at Erin.

"Then what are you doing farting around with us old gals? Off with you." Aunt Sophie waved her toward the door.

"You are not old by anyone's standards. I've seen you both turn a few young hotties' heads in your own right."

"Sophie's got herself a hottie."

"Really?" Erin asked her aunt. "That's great, Aunt Sophie."

"He's one of Mason's uncles."

"The man is head over heels." Maggie shook her head. "Imagine, every one of you matched up but me."

Sophie said, "Don't let her fool you. Her cell phone never stops ringing. Your mother breaks a heart a day and she mopes when the rest of us get lucky."

"Get lucky?" Maggie's eyes rounded. "There's no luck in the matter. And don't you act like you haven't been in and out of your own share of relationships." She turned to Erin. "Don't let your aunt fool you into thinking she's all innocent. She's just a little more low-key than I am."

Erin hugged them both. "I'd love to stay, but Jack

really is expecting me. I hope to get some work done today. I'll see you tomorrow."

"Bring this Jack by." Aunt Sophie nudged Maggie. "Help brighten up the place."

"I don't think I'm ready for that," Erin said as shivers of foreboding ran up her spine.

"It's okay, sweetheart." Maggie moved to her worktable and picked up a paintbrush. "We'd love to see you both if it works out. If not, don't worry about it."

"I'll stop by again soon."

"Okay, now scoot before the traffic gets bad." Aunt Sophie walked her to the door, but Maggie had already turned to the canvas near the window.

Erin slipped into her car. Sadness welled up inside her. How could Maggie lose her sight? It was so unfair. As the sorrow gripped her, thoughts of Jack drifted through her mind. No matter what else might be happening between the two of them, she needed him. She pushed her way through the early Friday traffic, anxious to reach him.

"JACK, YOU LOOK LIKE HELL. Is it your heart?" Amanda clapped her hand over his forehead. "Are you running a fever?"

He pushed her hand aside. "How did you get in?"

"The door was unlocked. I rang the bell."

"I guess I was dozing." He licked his dry lips. The

pounding in his head seemed to have subsided and the nausea had passed.

"Do I need to call someone? Your doctor?"

"Don't freak on me. I'm okay. It's just a little bug or something. I had it the other day, but it cleared up. Thought it was a twenty-four-hour thing. I'm fine. I'm feeling better."

"You're sure it isn't the other?"

"I'm sure. I spoke with my doctor's office earlier. Could you please get me some water and maybe some ibuprofen?"

"Sure." She left, returning a few moments later, shaking her head. "This is not a good thing, Jack. You scared the crap out of me. When I saw you lying there, all pale—"

"Stop. I'm okay. This is—" he took a sip of water "—temporary, whatever it is. Maybe I ate something that didn't agree with me."

"Should we call your doctor again, just to be sure?"

"They asked me a bunch of questions, then said to take it easy and call back if I'm still feeling bad in a few days, which I won't be. I'm much better already."

"Good." She sank to the edge of the bed. "How come you haven't returned my calls? You know that just makes me worry. I hate being the only one who knows what's going on with you. You need to talk to your mother about this. She should know.

Heaven forbid something should happen and there I am left to explain to one and all what a martyr you were."

Irritation grated through him. "I'm not a martyr and you know why I won't tell her."

"I know, but she would want to know."

"It'll only make her worry. She's been worrying enough already with the way I keep putting her off."

"You've started the weaning process," Amanda said. "You should have started years ago. It's harder because you've made yourself so indispensable."

"No one's indispensable. She's learning to stand on her own. I'm learning not to feel bad about that. At least she has Aunt Rose and Bobby."

"Right, they're so much help, because they also count on you to do everything. Bobby isn't the handyman you are and he doesn't spend the time with your mom that you do. But you're right. They'll learn to manage on their own. And you should not feel guilty. You've got all you can handle right now."

"Still, she's had enough grief. I hate to put anything else on her." He pushed himself into a sitting position, suddenly feeling better. "See? I'm fine." He yawned. "In fact, I feel pretty good."

"You're not as pale." She frowned. "You have got to start returning my calls. Don't make me worry like that again."

"Nothing is going to happen to me."

"That's not what your doctor says."

"He's obligated to point out risks. I understand what I'm up against and I'm taking care of it. I'm going to be fine." Thoughts of Erin drifted through his mind and the sense of peace and comfort that always accompanied her blanketed him. The energy that seemed to follow each bout of sickness coursed through him.

"You never told me how your hunt for a sexual healer went."

His stomach tightened. "She's much more than that."

"You met her?" Amanda's eyes rounded. "You punk. Now I'm really pissed you didn't call. Been busy, have you? Spill it."

"It's not like that. Erin's incredible. I *really* like her."

"You two get it on?"

"Mandy, that's none of your business."

"Oh, so you did. How was it?"

"I'm not discussing that with you. Look, she's going to be here any minute. Maybe you should leave."

"Hell, no. I want to meet her. One of the McClellan women. They're becoming legendary, you know." She socked him lightly in the arm. "I'm so proud." She frowned. "If you've been getting it on with her, why have you been sick? You sure this is the right woman?"

"Yes, but it doesn't matter who she is and I don't care about the sexual healing. Maybe you were wrong about her. She isn't into that."

"Doesn't matter whether she's into it or not. It's in her genes. She's got the power."

"I'm not denying she's got something. I don't know what it is, but it seems like magic to me." He rubbed his hand over his stubbled chin. "I didn't get squat done today. I'm going to have to log some time over the weekend. I should get cleaned up before she gets here." He gave her a pointed look.

"I'll stick around to let her in while you're busy then."

"She has a key."

"Isn't that a little fast?"

"I hired her to redesign the interior of this place. I'm not always going to be here when she needs to work, so I gave her a key."

"You hired her as an interior designer?"

"That's what I said."

"Isn't that going a little overboard?"

"Why? It's about time I did something with the place. I'm tired of staring at blank walls."

"But wouldn't it have been a lot cheaper to just date her?"

He gritted his teeth. "I didn't know what to do. You said to turn on my charm and let nature run its course, but it didn't work like that. I had to do something to strike up a relationship with her, so I hired her."

"I can't believe you're finally fixing up this place. You've lived here how long? I have to meet this woman."

"You don't need to meet her."

The doorbell sounded and he groaned as Amanda hopped from the bed to answer it. He hurried after her. "I'll get it."

But she was already pulling the door open. "Hi, you must be Erin." She extended her hand. "I'm Amanda. I'm a friend of Jack's."

"And she was just leaving." Jack pulled Erin up beside him and glared at Amanda.

"He's a little cranky. He wasn't feeling too well earlier, poor baby." Amanda patted his cheek.

"You've been ill?" Erin looked concerned. "Oh, Jack, I'm so sorry."

"I'm fine." He squeezed her shoulder. "How about you? I didn't give you a little intestinal bug or anything, did I?"

"No, I've been all right." She pressed her hand to his forehead. "Are you sure you're okay? You feel a little warm."

"I think he may have been doing some puking be-fore I got here."

"I was sleeping before she got here."

"But did you get sick?" Erin asked, her face drawn in worry.

"Not so bad this time."

"This time?"

"No big deal. I think I ate something that didn't agree with me the other night."

"When?"

"The other night, when you first came over."

"Oh." She stared at him, distraught.

Why was she so upset that he'd been ill? She looked stricken. Did it have something to do with her gift? Maybe she expected him to be vital and healthy after their sexual encounters, as Amanda had.

Guilt tightened his stomach. What if his condition prevented him from responding to her gift the way a healthier man would?

Her gaze drifted to Amanda. "It's nice to meet you, Amanda. I'm sorry Jack's been sick."

"Me, too, but he looks much better than he did when I first got here," Amanda said.

Erin squeezed his hand. Deep grooves marred her forehead. "Oh, dear."

Jack cleared his throat. "Amanda, don't you have that thing?"

"Oh, yeah, that…thing. It was nice meeting you, Erin. I see Jack's in good hands and you'll nurse him back to health."

Erin dropped his hand and stepped away from him. "Maybe I should leave."

"No." He scooped her back to his side. "You're staying. Amanda is leaving."

"That's right." Amanda stepped through the open door. "You two have fun. Jack, call me later."

They bid her goodbye, then shut the door. Erin turned to him. "Jack, I'm terribly sorry you've been ill."

He cupped her face, his gaze falling to her lips. God, she was beautiful. That she was this concerned over him filled him with warmth. "Baby, it's okay. I'm fine. In fact, I feel really energized."

Desire swirled around him. His body couldn't seem to get this close to her and not spontaneously combust. He brushed his lips across hers, aching for her kiss, but she pulled back.

"Jack—"

"Shh."

He kissed her.

She pressed her palm to his chest and pulled back. "No, Jack, we shouldn't."

His stomach clenched at the seriousness in her eyes. Had she forgotten how right it was between them? "Yes, we should."

He pulled her back and ran his lips over hers. Her hand pressed against him, but her lips softened beneath his. He had to remind her how good they were together. He teased his tongue along the crease of her lips, then slipped inside as she sighed. She resisted for the briefest moment, but then her body melted against him and she kissed him back, her arms slipping around his neck and her tongue dueling with his, stirring up the heat, sending his hormones soaring.

Before she could protest, he lifted her and carried her into the bedroom. At that moment, with her soft and pliant in his arms, her mouth hungry on his, he felt as though he could conquer the world. It was hard to believe he'd ever felt anything but vibrant and energetic. Every cell in his body came alive as she stroked her hand down his chest.

Whatever her magic, it was working. The last thing he meant to do was upset her over a passing malady that paled in significance beside the passion she aroused in him. He opened her blouse and blew on her rosy nipple before dipping his head to take her into his mouth. As he suckled her, he wondered about her upset over his illness. Her reaction—wanting to leave—seemed unwarranted, out of proportion.

He closed his eyes and his thoughts drifted as she moaned and moved beneath him, her fingers threading through his hair. He'd never get enough of her.

If he meant to keep her around as long as possible, there would be no more talk of illness.

One thing was clear—whatever happened, he could never tell her about his bad heart.

10

THE BUZZING OF HIS CELL PHONE roused Jack from a deep sleep. He opened one eye as the thing jumped across the dresser, then fell to the floor, where it buzzed some more. He scooped Erin closer and breathed in her musky scent. She'd been wild and un-inhibited last night. Every man's dream.

And she was his.

His stomach rumbled and he frowned, but the nausea stayed in check. Funny, he'd been sick again in the middle of the night. Thankfully Erin had slept through this round and he'd managed to recover fairly quickly. Whatever this bug was, it seemed to come and go. Maybe he should schedule an appointment with his doctor for next week, just to be on the safe side.

Erin murmured something in her sleep and pressed her bottom against him. He hardened almost immediately. If he was sick, it sure as hell wasn't af-fecting his cock. He nuzzled her neck while cupping her breast and drawing circles around her nipple with his thumb.

She made a soft sighing sound and arched so that her sex, already swollen and damp, rubbed his thigh. He traced the shell of her ear with his tongue and slipped his hand over the tight swell of her ass, up along the crease of her thigh, over her soft folds, where he lingered long enough to dip his fingers inside her before spreading her wetness over her clit.

Heat curled through him. She again moaned softly but did not come fully awake. He continued to stroke her, and she shifted so the tip of his cock brushed her slick entrance. He sucked in a breath and stilled, his every effort focused on not pressing into her. She was hot and aroused and lusciously asleep.

She moved again, more insistently, and he nearly slipped inside her. With the last thread of his senses he grabbed a condom off the nightstand. His hands unsteady, he tore open the packet, then readied himself.

For one quick moment he let his gaze drink in the sight of her tight ass and her pink flesh, so ready for him he ached with the need to take her. When she undulated against the bed, he gripped her by the hip and in one tantalizingly slow thrust seated himself deep inside her. He stopped for a moment to steady himself. If he was to wake her like this, he should do it gently. But she moaned and pressed back against him, and the pressure of her inner muscles tightening around him shredded the last of his control.

He thrust into her, the heat and tension spiraling through him. She gasped and her hand covered his as she came fully awake. "Jack."

"Erin." He cupped her breast as he continued to thrust in a rhythm that grew more frantic with each passing minute.

Her sexy cries urged him on as lights flashed all around and the heat seared him. Her body stiffened and she cried out as she came, her muscles rippling around him, squeezing him in the most intimate caress. With one final thrust he came, swallowing the triumphant yell that burned in his chest.

For long moments he lay spent, spooning her. She clasped her hands over his, her breasts heaving with her exertion, a pretty flush staining her skin. He kissed the nape of her neck. "Good morning."

Smiling, she rolled over to face him, her eyes still sleep-filled. "Good morning."

He let his gaze drift over her. Her eyes were as green as glass, her lovely breasts rosy and beaded, her lips smiling dreamily. He traced his thumb over her full bottom lip. "You were rubbing against me when I woke up. I couldn't help myself."

"You don't hear me complaining."

His stomach clenched and he frowned as the nausea hit him again. He gave her a quick kiss on the forehead. "I'm a mess. Let me get cleaned up."

She traced her finger across his chest. "Want some company?"

"Uh, give me a few minutes?"

His cell phone buzzed again from its place on the carpet, vibrating against the bottom of the dresser with a rattling sound. Erin frowned and sat up, seeming to come more fully awake. Her eyes rounded in alarm. "Jack, are you okay?"

"Feeling great. I'll be right back." With a forced smile he retrieved his cell phone from the floor as he bypassed the adjoining bathroom and headed for the one down the hall.

She tucked the sheet around her, worry etched into her face. "I'll be here waiting."

He nodded and hurried down the hall, bile rising in his throat and his stomach spasming. Clutching the phone, he turned on the water, then heaved into the toilet. This was getting ridiculous.

What the hell? How could he feel so off-the-wall fantastic one minute, then so wretched the next? He heaved again, his stomach twisting.

Within a few moments the attack had passed. He pressed his hand to his chest, and his heart beat steady and strong beneath his palm. Well, there was that.

Strange, the illness came and went more quickly

with each occurrence. Maybe that meant he was getting over whatever it was. After he'd cleaned himself and aired out the bathroom, he checked his cell phone.

His brother had called. Twice. He hit the button to return the call, then waited through several rings before Bobby picked up. "Yo, Jack, where you been?"

"I've been…busy. What's up, Bobby?"

"Aren't you coming over here? I can't do this on my own. You know how hard today is for her."

Shit. It was Saturday already, the twelfth of November. How had he let that sneak up on him? "Yeah, I'm coming. I…uh…have someone here. Let me see what's going on and then I'll get there as quickly as I can."

"Man, hurry, she's already started with the food. She's been baking since last night."

"Tell her I'm on my way if she asks."

"*If* she asks? Who do you think had me call you?"

Jack wrapped a towel around his waist as he hurried to find Erin. She wasn't in the bedroom, the master bath or the kitchen. A rustling pointed him in the direction of the living room, where he found her.

She'd dressed in the clothes she'd worn last night. Papers and books surrounded her, as well as a ring of fabric swatches. She didn't glance up as he entered. "How are you, Jack? Are you feeling okay? Did you have a touch of…that bug you had before?"

"No, nothing like that." He hated lying to her, but she seemed so upset by the prospect of him being ill, it seemed the better way to go. "How are you?"

She nodded and busied herself over the pad she'd used to take notes the other night. "Just thought now might be a good time to get started."

"It's Saturday, Erin. Are you sure you want to work today?"

Her gaze remained fastened on her notes. Her voice sounded strained. "This project is going to take some doing. Better to get started so I can wrap it up in a decent amount of time."

His stomach tightened. "Baby, what's wrong?"

She still did not look at him. "Nothing. I just have a lot to do. I want to finish drawing these plans for you to look over before I get started and I'm sure you have…things to do, too."

"I do. I have to go somewhere. I have to see my family."

"That's nice. I have to go see mine later this afternoon. You don't mind if I stick around and work a little first?"

"No. That's fine." He stood for a minute, torn. He should get moving, but she seemed upset about something. He couldn't leave her like this. He reached for her. "Hey, weren't we going to shower together?"

She flinched away from him, her gaze directed at the floor. "I don't think that's such a good idea."

"Why not?" He knelt beside her. "Baby, tell me what's bothering you. Did I do something?"

"No, it's not you. It's me. You touch me and I lose my head. I should just go."

"Don't. Please, Erin, don't run away from this. I want to be with you. I lose control when we're together, too. Why is that a bad thing? The chemistry is that strong between us. It's not anyone's fault. That's the way it is, and we're damn lucky for it, if you ask me. I wouldn't give it up for anything."

"You don't understand. Last night—this morning—shouldn't have happened."

"Why the hell not?" He gestured toward his bedroom. "You can't tell me you didn't enjoy that every bit as much as I did."

"Enjoying it isn't the point." She gathered up her papers. "Look, I can't explain, but I think we need to take a break."

Anger and hurt warred in him. How could she find fault with what they had? "People would kill for the kind of passion we have. How can you not want that? Look me in the eye and tell me you really want this break and I'll go along with it."

She met his gaze and a single tear trailed down her cheek. "I want us to take a break."

He stared at her a long moment while his insides twisted. Whether it was some residual effect of his earlier attack or his body's response to her rejection didn't seem to matter. It hurt.

Hell.

"Why? I think I deserve to know that much. What did I do—or not do?" he asked.

She shook her head. "I told you, it isn't you. You've been great." Her voice shook. "If I tell you, you'll think I'm nuts."

"I think it's a little nuts to throw away what we have."

Red rimmed her eyes. "Great. Maybe I am crazy. That should be reason enough."

"You are not crazy."

"Remember when I told you about my nutso family? How they believe they're a bunch of sexual healers and how they think I'm one, too?"

He shrugged, unable to hold her gaze. "Maybe that's not so crazy. Maybe there's really something to it. I've had more energy since we've been together." And no dizziness or pains in his chest. "I've been feeling pretty good, actually."

"Have you really?"

He glanced up at her and the knot in his stomach tightened. "Well, yeah, for the most part."

"And what about this…this bug or whatever it is

that you've had? Have you noticed anything about the timing?"

"The timing? It's been off and on, but it always goes away. What do you mean?"

"Think about it, Jack. When do you get sick?"

"Hell, Erin, what are you getting at?"

"When do you get sick?"

He sat back on his heels, frowning. "The first time was Wednesday night."

"The first night we made love."

He shook his head. What was she saying? "The next time was the next night."

"After we made love again, right?"

"That's just a coincidence."

"We've been together for the past three nights and you've been sick each time, haven't you? Each time after we make love."

"That's crazy. People don't get sick from sleeping with each other."

"Oh, but it's not a stretch to say people get healed by sleeping together?"

His face warmed. "Okay, that's a stretch, too."

"Jack, this isn't the first time."

"What do you mean?"

"This has happened before. At first I thought it was some weird coincidence, too, but it kept happening. And always after I had sex with a guy. It's me."

"You?" He blinked at her.

"Yes, me. I'm Typhoid Mary reincarnated. Maybe I really do come from a long line of sexual healers, but if so, then something went wrong in the gene pool when I came along.

"I didn't mean to be with you," she said. "It just kind of happened and then I thought that you were okay, that maybe because you didn't get sick right away in front of me like the others that maybe you'd be different—immune somehow. Last night when your friend Amanda was here and she started talking about you being sick…I knew then that we couldn't be together. But you touched me and I can't keep a straight thought in my head when you're touching me. I…"

"Erin." He touched her arm. The thrill that always ran through him when he held her—when her skin touched his—was still there. "I don't know about any of that, but I do know that when I'm with you, the world suddenly makes sense. How could you be making me sick when touching you, being with you, is the only magic I have ever experienced?"

"I have to go." Her voice was soft, tormented. She rose, clutching her belongings, and headed for the door. She glanced back at him before she left. "Goodbye, Jack. I'll be back to work the redesign, like we agreed."

He stared at the closed door after she'd gone. How could she believe such a thing? They'd work it out. At least she'd be back. He'd convince her later that she was mistaken.

For now, he had to get to his mother's house, where he would gorge himself on all of his sister's favorite foods that his mom made…for his sister who had died seven years ago to this day.

WHAT WAS WRONG WITH HER? Erin stopped in her living room. Her quiet, normal living room with every throw pillow and magazine in place. Her lonely living room in her lonely apartment.

Who was she kidding? She'd never have a normal life. Normal lives were for normal people. She slept with men and made them ill. That was not normal.

She dropped her things on the coffee table, then headed for the shower. And she'd made Jack sick. Poor, sweet, unsuspecting Jack. When Amanda had said he'd been sick, Erin had known she needed to break things off with him.

But then he'd kissed her and she'd been lost. She should have resisted him, for his own good. The thought of him being ill because of her mortified her. How many times had she let him take her last night? Heat filled her at the flood of memories. And then this morning, she'd dreamed of making love to him, of him touching her, slipping inside her.

But it hadn't been a dream.

She turned the shower on hot, stripped, then stepped under the spray. Memories of her shower with Jack flowed over her. Her skin tingled. Her nipples beaded.

Why did she have to be tainted? It was so unfair. Maybe she would have been okay with being the only McClellan without the gift of sexual healing. But this? This was some kind of cruel joke.

Jack might say he wanted her now, but how long would he be able to take it? Who wanted a woman with the power to twist a man's insides until he retched?

Stupid, stupid woman.

She'd known better than to get involved with him. How could she have such poor restraint? She had to finish his condo as quickly as possible.

Maybe they could work out a schedule where they weren't there at the same time. Jack worked from home some, but he spent a good amount of time out in the field and in clients' offices. Maybe the best way to stay out of his bed would be to stay clear of him. She'd call him later to work out the details.

Her heart heavy, she finished washing, then dressed in jeans and a T-shirt. The light on her answering machine blinked. She pressed the message button.

"Hey, sweet girl, this is Thomas. I understand you need some help installing some halogen lights for your mom. I'm going to head over there. I promised Maggie I'd come play gin, so I'll be there whenever you can make it. See you soon."

She let the message erase. How could she have thought Jack might be her Thomas? Obviously the only reason Thomas was still around after all these years was because he'd stayed out of Maggie's bed. None of the rest of Maggie's lovers had had any staying power, not even Erin's or her sisters' fathers.

The afternoon was well worn by the time she picked up the lights from her shop, then headed for Aunt Sophie's. When she arrived, Tess's car sat in the drive. Erin closed her eyes. Tess and her exuberance for life were always a little hard to take. Today would be even harder.

"There's my other girl." Thomas answered the door, a mug in his hand. He gave her a quick hug. "We were wondering when you'd get here. Come help me. Your mother is whipping my ass."

"I'm not much of a gin player."

"We're playing crazy eights." Tess slapped an oversize card on the stack in the middle of the table.

Maggie sat across from her and Aunt Sophie sat beside her at the massive oak table in the kitchen. As always, something herb-scented sizzled in the oven and Aunt Sophie's ever-present teapot sat on the stove.

"Hi, honey." Maggie patted her arm. "Come on, join us. We can deal you in the next round."

"That's okay. I'm going to get the lights out of my trunk and get started on that."

"I'll help you." Thomas said.

"No, Thomas, it's all right. I can do simple wiring. I'll need to throw the breaker, but the kitchen is probably not going to be affected."

"You sure, honey? I don't mind helping." Thomas asked.

"I'll call you if I need you."

"Wait, don't run off without a cup of tea." Aunt Sophie handed her a cup. "There, with cream and sugar, just how you like it. Oh, and take a honey cake. It'll tide you over until dinner's ready." She handed Erin a plate with a small square of cake.

"I don't know if I'm staying for dinner."

"Of course you are, dear. Maggie's cooking a pot roast, and you know how she likes to overdo. The thing is humongous. You have to help us eat it or we'll be eating leftovers for weeks to come."

"We'll see." Erin sipped the tea. As usual, it was a blend she didn't recognize but surprisingly hearty for a tea. She breathed in the steam and her spirits lifted. "This is good, Aunt Sophie."

"Just something I brewed especially for you. I had a feeling you'd need something with an extra kick to it today." She tucked a strand of Erin's hair behind her ear. "Always go with your gut, dear."

"Sure." Erin raised the mug in salute, then headed toward Maggie's studio.

Aunt Sophie had some strange ideas. Erin shook her head. She would have to think about that one. Right now her gut was so twisted she had no idea what it was telling her.

Thomas checked on her an hour later and helped her sort out the last of the wiring on the track lights she'd brought. By then Erin's stomach was growling mercilessly. The tea and honey cake had done little to satisfy her hunger. It seemed she'd been hungry ever since she'd met Jack Langston.

"I'm hungry, too," Thomas responded to a particularly loud rumble from her stomach. "I think dinner's ready. You're staying, aren't you?"

"I guess so. I skipped lunch." She threw the new dimmer switch they'd installed and stepped back to assess her handiwork. "Better, don't you think?"

"Definitely. She should be pleased, though truth be told, I don't know that it will help for much longer."

"She's getting worse."

"She doesn't read or drive anymore. And did you

see the size of those cards? Sophie found them in a novelty shop." He heaved a big sigh. "But Maggie has a great attitude. I think it helps she knows we're all there for her. Let me show you what I got her before we join the others." He pulled a bundle from the cabinet above Maggie's workbench. He opened it to reveal a huge square of gray clay. "It's sculptor's clay."

"Didn't she take a sculpting class once a long time ago?"

"You and Tess were just starting school. The two of you would get into it sometimes and we'd find this stuff all over the place."

Erin smiled as the memory washed over her. Sometimes she forgot all the good times from her childhood. It was nice to be reminded. "I'd forgotten. She liked it, didn't she—the sculpting?"

"Maggie likes anything having to do with art. She likes to paint better, but I figured this might be easier for her as she goes along."

"What did she say when you gave it to her?"

"She said thank you, then shoved it in the cabinet. But I know she'll bring it out one of these days. She's still painting." He gestured toward the covered canvas near the window. "Some days go better than others. When she has an off painting day, maybe she'll turn to the clay. I want her to know she has options."

The tenderness in his voice sent a ripple of warmth

through Erin. If she ever found a man to love her the way Thomas loved Maggie, she'd count herself blessed.

"I'm so glad she has you, Thomas."

"Yeah, me, too. Hell, I'm not going anywhere."

Her stomach made another protest that had them both laughing. Thomas escorted her to the kitchen, where the rest of them had cleared away the cards and were indeed setting out a mouthwatering spread of pot roast, mashed potatoes, carrots and green beans.

"Have a seat." Maggie placed a basket smelling of warm bread on the table in front of Erin.

"That smells too good to resist," Erin said as she took one of the soft rolls.

Tess settled beside her and passed her the butter as the rest took their seats. "Filling up on those carbs, I see. Is my little sister still sporting a big appetite?"

Ignoring her, Erin nearly moaned in ecstasy as she bit into the buttered roll. "This is incredible. Aunt Sophie, did you make these?"

"That I did. I popped them out of the freezer, into the oven."

Thomas passed Erin a platter of the sliced beef. "Here you go, hon, try some of this."

The clink of dishes and the scrape of silverware

filled the air as everyone heaped healthy portions on their plates. Sophie said a quiet blessing and then they all dug in.

"This is better than Thanksgiving," Thomas said as he sliced the tender meat. "You ladies aren't trying to fatten me up?"

"Heaven's no, Thomas," Sophie said. "We want you trim and agile enough to climb up on that roof to clean the gutters."

"Is it that time again?" he asked.

Tess leaned forward. "Aunt Sophie, what would you and Maggie do without Thomas?"

"We would have to pack it in, right, Maggie?"

Maggie placed her hand over Thomas's. "I, for one, never intend to find out. You're never leaving me, isn't that right, Thomas?"

"I don't think anyone else will have me, Mags. I'm getting too old to find me a young miss. Guess you're stuck with me," he said.

Laughter sounded around the table and Erin relaxed. Maybe her family wasn't so very different from other families all across America sitting down to share the evening meal.

"So, Erin, who is this new mystery man you're seeing?" Tess asked.

Warmth filled Erin's cheeks. "I'd rather not talk about it."

Disappointment swirled in Tess's blue eyes. "You mean you dumped him already."

"Now wait a minute," Sophie said. "You don't know how the gift works with your sister. Maybe it was time for her young man to move on. Just because your men had a tendency to linger doesn't mean Erin's men will stick around the same way."

"I understand that. And just because the gift works one way at one time, doesn't mean that it will continue to work in that same way. Look how Nikki's and mine changed for us." Tess laughed. "She couldn't keep a man until morning until she met Dylan, who's planning on being there for good."

"And then there's you and Mason," Maggie said.

"Right. It was the opposite for me. I had all my guys and they stayed around forever, until I met Mason and then, poof, they were gone."

"But you still have Mason." Maggie's eyes glistened.

"Yes, I still have Mason."

"How is he?" Erin asked, grateful the conversation had veered away from her and Jack and hoping Tess would drop the matter.

"He's doing great. He's at the free clinic today. Project Mentor has found some land and the board is reviewing the plans for the youth center. Looks like it's all coming to fruition."

"That's wonderful, honey." Maggie smiled. "The two of you must be very happy."

"We are."

"When's he going to make an honest woman of you?" Thomas asked.

"This is Nikki's time. I'm in no hurry. It'll happen when it happens."

"But you've talked about it?" Aunt Sophie prompted.

Pink tinged Tess's cheeks. "Constantly. It's becoming a regular topic of conversation."

"So what's the problem?" Sophie asked. "You know Nikki would be thrilled to make this a double wedding. Think of how you could split all the costs."

"I don't care about a big wedding as long as my family is all there. To me, we're already living together. We're both committed to this relationship. A piece of paper isn't going to change that."

"Maybe it will for Mason." Sophie reached across the table for the basket of rolls. "Then there's the possibility of having children. Have you talked about that?"

Erin set aside her fork. All this talk of weddings and children seemed to kill her appetite. Would she ever have any of that?

"Mason wants children," Tess said. "He wants four, actually, but we've compromised at two. I would love to have a girl and a boy, but I'll be happy to just have two healthy kids."

"Oh, a baby." Maggie clasped her hands to her breast. "Wouldn't it be just lovely to have a little one about again?" She turned to Tess. "Please say you're planning this soon."

Tess squeezed her hand. "Mom, we're just starting to talk about all this. I'm not sure I'm ready to have a child. I've just gotten used to the Project Mentor teens. Truly the thought of having a little helpless baby in my care twenty-four hours a day, seven days a week, scares the crap out of me."

"But we'll help. You can drop the baby here while you and Mason are at work. Right, Sophie?"

"Sure, drop the little monster off and we'll take care of it."

"There, that's settled." Maggie beamed. "So will it be a double wedding or do you prefer to have your own ceremony?"

"Whoa, slow down. I promise I will talk some more with Mason…and…I'll let you know if and when there's anything to know."

"Another wedding." Maggie said. "How marvelous. And Erin has her young man. All my girls are happy."

Sophie shrugged in a matter-of-fact way. "Of course they're happy. They each have the gift. Happiness and a life of love are all part of it."

Erin bit her lip. She should say something. She should set them straight. Again the feelings of betrayal swept over her. Somehow accepting the gift seemed to diminish all the tormented memories of never having a real home, of being taunted by classmates and of never having her own family understand her. But these things *had* happened and the memory of them stung. Why couldn't they go back to the days when she'd been oblivious to their family heritage?

They all thought she had the gift. She sat at the table with them and she was certainly related to them according to her birth certificate, but she had never felt like a real member of this family. She was different from them. She was a fraud. As far as being a true McClellan, she was faking it.

11

"JACK!" GRACE LANGSTON swept her arms around her son and held him close. "I was worried. I thought you might not make it."

"You knew I'd come." Jack pulled back to look at his mother.

Wisps of hair had escaped the ponytail that held her honey-blond hair. Though worry lines marked her brow, her eyes were the same bright blue they'd always been and her figure just as trim. At fifty-one she was still a beautiful woman.

He brushed a sprinkle of flour from her cheek. "Bobby said you were cooking up a storm—that we'd need an army to eat it all."

"Well, you know how it is when the mood strikes me." She turned toward the counter and stove top crammed with dishes and pots of varying sizes, each issuing an aroma to tempt the appetite.

He lifted a lid and stirred the creamy pasta and vegetables. "Chicken alfredo."

"And there's beef stroganoff, in case you have a taste for that instead, and green-bean casserole, a Caesar salad, those little crescent rolls Stacey used to love and then there's all the desserts." She gestured to another counter that held a cake of some sort, a pie and a plate of brownies.

"Mom, this is a lot of food. Maybe more than usual. Is everything okay?"

She nodded, her lips pressed together. "Do you remember that sweet Alex Carver Stacey used to have over every now and then? She had the biggest crush on you for a while."

"I remember Alex."

"I ran into her in the grocery store the other day. She had a cart full of groceries, a huge diamond on her finger and the most beautiful baby girl riding in a carrier in the basket. She was such an angel, Jack. I wish you could have seen her."

"Stacey would be—what?—twenty-three. Isn't that young to have a child?"

"I was twenty-two when I had you."

He wrapped his arm around her and pulled her to his side. "And it made you think of Stacey and what it might have been like had she lived."

She nodded again, her lips pressed tightly together, her eyes misting. "It's hard not to wonder. Would she have married? Had children? Been happy?"

He didn't say anything. What could take away the pain of losing a child? He still mourned his sister.

Sometimes it was hard to believe she'd really been gone all these years, especially here in the house where they'd grown up together. The house where they'd lived when his father had died. This place had seen so much grief. Too much.

He kissed his mother's hair. "Hey, I have an idea. Do you ever think about selling this place—moving somewhere new?"

She sighed and pulled away from him to stir one of the pots on the stove. "I've thought about it, yes. Your aunt Rose and I have talked about it from time to time and we even once went out with a real-estate agent and looked around."

"Really? You didn't find anything?"

"Oh, there was this cute little place in Pembrook Pines we both liked. We thought about it, but…"

"You didn't want to leave."

She glanced at him and tears glistened in her eyes. "I have so many memories here of all of us, of Stacey and your father. Yes, sometimes, like today, it's hard. Sometimes it almost seems as though one of them might come walking through that door. I know they won't, but here in this house, it's like I still have a small part of them."

She put the lid back on the pot and turned to him. "Does that make sense?"

"Sure it does."

"Jack, I know how busy you've been lately, but I lost the number to that handyman. Besides, you know how I always fret about having a strange man here."

"He's a good man, Mom. I wouldn't have recommended him otherwise."

"Of course not. I'm sorry."

Guilt filled him. "What needs fixing? I'll look at it after dinner."

A smile lit her face. "Thank you, dear. It's the garage door. It's been getting stuck."

"I'll take care of it, Mom."

Was it so bad to help her? He'd pick up his plan to be less indispensable later. He couldn't turn his back on her now. Not today.

"You've been so unavailable lately. I was afraid to ask."

His stomach tightened. "You do need to learn to take care of these things yourself. I can't always be here for you."

"I know. I shouldn't depend on you so much. It's a bad habit."

He kissed her cheek. "No worries, Mom. I'm here now. No reason why I can't help out."

"Thank God I have you, Jack." She washed her

hands, then wiped them on a dish towel. "Everything's ready. Why don't you go get your aunt and your brother? They were in the den watching whatever game's on today."

As Jack took out the trash later that evening, he stared up at the night sky and cursed silently to himself. The tightening in his chest had returned and had gotten worse throughout the night.

He stifled the impulse to call Erin, though he longed just to hold her again. He needed to give her at least the night to calm down and think. Surely she didn't believe she actually made men sick.

She had the magic.

He felt it every time he was with her. If for some reason the sickness accompanied her magic, then so be it. He'd ralph a thousand times to be with her once. She was worth it.

He turned to go into the house. It was late. He needed to get home and get some rest. The day had been stressful, first with Erin, then his mother and this house with all its memories. He needed to go home and catch some shut-eye, give his body a chance to mend.

In the morning he'd talk to Erin. He hadn't had trouble with his heart the entire time he'd been with her. She definitely had the magic. Every cell of his being felt the truth in that. Maybe if she came back, she could truly heal him. Then he wouldn't have to tell his mother, who'd already lost first a husband, then a daughter, that her son might be next.

"HI." ERIN SCOOTED OVER on the porch swing as Tess settled beside her.

Crickets chirped in the night air and a car rolled by along the quiet street. Tess spread one of Aunt Sophie's big shawls around both of them to stave off the slight chill. "Thought you had left."

"I would have said goodbye."

"That's good to know, considering that none of us knew you were moving until after the fact. Then you moved way up there past Boca. If we were sensitive types, we might think you were getting as far away from the rest of us as you could."

"Good thing you're not the sensitive type then."

They sat in silence for a moment. Erin pushed against the floorboard to set the swing rocking. "I was going to leave, but it was so nice out here."

"I have always loved Aunt Sophie's house. There were times when we were growing up when I wanted us to live here."

"Me, too. But we practically did anyway."

"Not quite," Tess said. "We always had to leave eventually. You probably don't remember, but Nikki used to pitch the biggest fits."

"She always wanted a home like this."

"Well, now she has it."

"And so do you." A feeling of wretchedness stole over Erin. She gazed off up the street. "So you and Mason will probably tie the knot, too."

"I think so."

"Why haven't you said yes?"

"I don't know exactly. I'm sure I will. We have a life plan to stick together through thick and thin. I feel like we're already married."

"So you'll say yes when you're ready to have children?"

"I think so, though Mom never felt marriage was a necessity along those lines. I think we turned out okay, thanks to Thomas and Aunt Sophie, but there's no way Mason is going to have children with me if I don't marry him first."

"I like Mason. I'm truly happy for you."

Tess's smile was full of affection. "Thanks." She nudged Erin. "So how about you? Is this guy Mr. Right or Mr. Right Now?"

"You're going to keep asking until I tell you about him, aren't you?"

"I just want my baby sister to be happy. Is that so bad?"

"I don't think I can be happy in the sense you and Nikki are," Erin said.

"That's not true. We've both proven that the gift doesn't keep us from settling down with just one man. It's happened with Nikki and me. There's no reason it can't happen with you. It's just a matter of finding the right partner to channel your particular energy."

"The right conduit."

"Exactly, which brings me to another closely related subject. I think I know how we can help Mom," Tess said.

"How?"

"Thomas. He's the right conduit."

"Thomas? What are you saying?" Erin asked.

"I'm saying that I believe Thomas can heal Maggie's sight."

"Thomas? He's a healer?"

"No, he's the right conduit, like you said. This is just a theory, but I think it will work. Nikki and I have been talking about it and she thinks the same thing." Tess gave the swing another push.

"You two are always cooking something up. I'm not sure I want to be a part of this."

"Not even if it will fix her optic nerves or whatever is failing in there? Have you noticed how sometimes she gets that unfocused look? I think it's getting worse."

"She stumbled on the stairs when I brought her

home the other day. It really upset her. She said she's taking classes for the visually impaired."

"That tears me up. Don't you want to do something?" Tess asked.

"Of course I do, but I don't see how you think Thomas is the answer."

"There's always been a thing between them. I've never really understood it," Tess said. "She goes off with all these other men. They have never slept together, but he's always there for her."

"I know. I want a Thomas. Do you think he's been with other women since he's met Maggie, though? I hate to think he hasn't."

"I remember once they were arguing and Aunt Sophie said it was because Mom didn't approve of someone he was seeing, so I think he has, but he's kept it quiet. I don't think he's seeing anyone now. I put out some feelers earlier."

"Okay, but none of that says why you think he can help."

"Well, when you're with a guy sexually, you know how that empathic thing happens and you can feel what he's feeling?"

Irritation grated through Erin. "You're assuming I experience the gift like you do."

"I know it's different for all of us, but you know what I'm saying."

Yes, with Jack, Erin had felt it. "I guess so."

"See, I think—and Nikki agrees—that since there seems to be this reciprocal emotional thing happening, then there can also be this reciprocal healing. The healer in some cases, with the right man, becomes the healee, healed in essence by her own gift, intensified through her lover, someone who loves her like no other."

Erin sighed. "It sounds incredibly romantic, but I don't know. This is all a lot of conjecture."

"But what can it hurt? They have a deep and abiding love for each other. One doesn't breathe without the other knowing about it. They have everything going except for the sex."

"But maybe there's a reason for that. Like they aren't attracted to each other in that way."

"I'm not so sure. I've seen how they look at each other sometimes. I can't believe that in all these years they haven't thought about it."

"So what are you proposing?" Erin asked, knowing she didn't want to hear the answer.

"That we nudge them into an affair."

"How?"

"A romantic setting, candlelight, soft music, a bottle of wine. I don't know. What do you think?"

"I think we should think about the consequences. What if we get them to hook up, your theory's a bust and then they split up because it's too weird and we never see Thomas again. Sex can ruin a relationship. Believe me, I know."

"But I don't think that's going to happen," Tess insisted.

"You have no way of telling. And you're gambling with Maggie's happiness."

"That's right, it's a gamble to hopefully save her eyesight and to maybe—just maybe—help her find her one true love. The one who's been right there in front of her from the beginning. Isn't it worth a shot?"

A mixture of emotions swirled through Erin: worry that they might be doing the wrong thing, uncertainty about the possible outcome and an unquenchable hope that Tess could be right, not just for Maggie and Thomas but for all of them. If something this wondrous could work for her mother, then could it be that she herself had some chance at happiness?

She turned to Tess. "When do we try it?"

"I don't know. How about now? Aunt Sophie's in the kitchen brewing up whatever she brews. I think they're watching TV. We could go in and mess with the lights and the setting." She stood. Excitement shone in her eyes. "Come on, we'll figure it out as we go."

Erin rose to trail after her. "Seduction on a wing and a prayer. This should be interesting."

"ERIN, IT'S JACK. PLEASE pick up. I've thought about what you said and I don't know if it's true or not, but it doesn't matter." He pressed his hand to where the vise gripped his chest. "All I know is that I've felt like hell since you walked out of here yesterday and all I want is for you to come back. Please, baby, give me a call."

He hung up and stared at the phone in his hand. A night of rest hadn't done him much good. Not that he'd been able to sleep. The bed was too big and empty, and Erin's scent covered the sheets.

Where was she? What was she doing? If she didn't call soon, he might have to drive over to her apartment to look for her.

His doorbell sounded. His pulse quickened. Could it be Erin? He strode to yank open the door, but Amanda stood on his step.

She pushed inside past him, into the living room. "You look like hell."

"You know, Amanda, that isn't the best way to greet a guy."

"It's true. You look worse than you did the other day, and that was pretty bad. What's up? Still sick with that bug?"

"No."

She moved in front of him, frowning. "Why don't

you sit down? I'll get you some juice or something. What do you have?"

"There's orange juice that should be fairly drinkable."

"I'll check the expiration date." She moved off into the kitchen, where she banged around for a few moments before returning with two glasses. She handed him one. "It's still good."

"Thanks." He sipped the cold drink and it did feel good going down. Had he eaten today?

Pressing his hand to his chest, he eased into one of the living room chairs. "Take a load off."

"I'm on my way to power walk along South Beach. You up for it?"

"I probably should, but I'll take a rain check today."

She frowned. "Your ticker's acting up again, isn't it? Do I need to call someone?"

"I'm fine." He grated the words through clenched teeth. "Just having an off day."

"Sorry. Sure you shouldn't take something?"

"I took my meds this morning. I'll be okay. Just need to take it easy."

"Okay. So yesterday was D-day, wasn't it? I forgot, but I had it marked on my calendar."

D-day was her abbreviation for Death Day. "It's probably pretty twisted that we get together for a big feast on those days, but Mom gets so melancholy, and when she feels that way she cooks and bakes."

"So how was it?"

"She ran into a friend of Stace's who's married and has a kid. She took it pretty hard. Can't seem to stop all the what-ifs."

"I'm sorry, Jack." She squeezed his arm. "At least she has the rest of you there for her."

"Yeah, for now." He patted her hand. "Sorry, I didn't mean that."

"Yes, you did. You're really worried about your heart, aren't you?"

"I may call the doctor tomorrow and talk to him again about the surgery."

"It's getting worse?"

He shrugged. "I'm damned if I do and damned if I don't. Either I get the surgery and put everyone through the hell of worrying I'll end up like Stacey, or I ignore it like my old man did and wait for it to cut me down one day out of the blue."

"What about your sexual healer? What's happening with her?"

"I'm not sure." He shook his head. "She kind of dumped me yesterday."

"I'm not so sure that's a bad thing. She wasn't what I'd expected."

"How so?"

"I don't know. She didn't seem to have that healing vibe. I pictured her all in control and serene, but she seemed almost distraught. So she dumped you and you're feeling bad. Let's look at the other alternatives. What about magnetic therapy? I was reading about that the other day and I think it might be worth a shot."

"I don't want to try any more whacked-out alternative therapies. I want Erin. She has the magic touch. Maybe I got a little sick each time, but then I'd feel great—better than great—and I didn't have a single problem with my heart the whole time we were together."

"You think she made you sick? I don't know, Jack. I don't think she's so good for you. You haven't looked that great these past few days. Maybe her healing magic isn't working with you and your heart doesn't need the extra strain. Maybe it would be best to cut your losses in this case."

He didn't answer, just stared at the phone in his hand. He hadn't realized he was still holding it. Had she gotten his message yet?

"I'm going to head out, unless you need me to stick around," Amanda said.

"No, you go ahead. Enjoy the beach. I'll catch you next time." He walked her out, then headed back to his bed. The room swam around him and he collapsed in a heap, a dull pain in his chest.

12

ERIN PAUSED OUTSIDE Jack's door the following afternoon. She felt horrible. Not only had she screwed up everything with Jack by sleeping with him, but also she'd let Tess talk her into that ridiculous plot to set up Thomas and Maggie.

What a disaster that had been. Maggie had caught on to them before they'd gotten the candles lit. Needless to say, she'd been none too pleased with their meddling.

Now Erin had to face her situation with Jack—or at least figure out how to tie up his project in record time, then get the hell out of Dodge. She'd had good reason to set that policy of not dating clients.

She'd called and he hadn't answered, so hopefully he wasn't home. She couldn't face him right now.

She pulled out the key he'd given her, then opened the door. She'd take some measurements, then she'd be able to finish up the plans she'd started for him.

The house was quiet as she'd hoped. Jack didn't seem to be around. "Hello? Jack? Anyone here?"

She listened for a minute, then pulled her tape measure from her purse, as well as her pen and notebook, and set her things on the coffee table. Tape measure in hand, she marked the dimensions of the room, then recorded them in her notebook.

As she headed into the next room, words from the message Jack had left on her answering machine drifted over her.

All I know is that I've felt like hell since you walked out of here yesterday and all I want is for you to come back.

How many times had she picked up the phone to call him? She'd replayed that message at least a dozen times just to hear his voice. But she hadn't called and here she was sneaking around while he was gone.

She laid down the tape measure, then walked the length of the formal dining room, doing her best to focus on the job at hand. She had to tie this project up as quickly as possible. She'd found some great artwork for this room, if Jack agreed to the color scheme she'd chosen.

She recorded the dimensions of the dining room, then moved on to the kitchen. She should finish up pretty quickly. Still, thoughts of him crowded her mind.

What had he meant when he'd said he'd felt like hell since she walked out? Did he mean emotionally or physically?

Memories of her last morning with him rolled over her. Waking from that wet dream to find it wasn't a dream at all. She closed her eyes and pushed the memory away. She couldn't think about that now. Jack had probably paid dearly for that little bit of heaven.

At least he'd been well enough to go out. Whatever illness may have visited him after they'd made love was hopefully short-lived. As far as any emotional discomfort she may have caused him, surely that would be short-lived, as well. He'd get over her. Just as she'd get over him.

Eventually.

She measured the kitchen, then moved down the hall toward his bedroom. How could she work in there with all those memories of him hanging about? She squinted into the darkened room. He hadn't made the bed or opened the blinds.

She moved to the window. A little sunlight wouldn't hurt the place. She'd change these blinds for a nice set of drapes.

With a twist of her fingers she flooded the room with daylight. A movement from the bed startled her. She turned, her hand to her heart. Jack struggled to his side to blink at her, his eyes bleary and filled with pain.

"Oh, my God, Jack." She rushed to him, her stomach twisting at the sight of him. "What's happened? What have I done to you?"

He clasped her hand, his grip weak. "It wasn't you, baby."

"Then what? What's wrong?" She smoothed her hand over his cheek, her heart breaking over his obvious pain. "What's hurting you, Jack?"

"My…heart."

"Your heart? What's wrong?" Alarm raced up her spine. She looked around for his phone. "We should call someone. Are you having a heart attack?"

He shook his head. "I have a bad ticker. I was born with it. It's been acting up a little lately."

"What do I do? Do you have pills or something?" Her own heart thudded. Panic gripped her.

He grimaced and squeezed her hand. "I'm so glad you came. We need to talk."

"We will. We'll talk all you want, but we have to take care of you first. I'm going to call your doctor, okay?"

He nodded.

"Where's his number?"

"In my wallet, on the dresser. Dr. Carmichael." He closed his eyes.

Erin frantically scanned the contents of his wallet until she found the card. "Phone, where's the phone?"

She tossed aside clothes and bed coverings until she unearthed the phone. She tried the number three times before she punched it in correctly. Her pulse pounded in her ears as she waited through four rings.

Finally a recording answered and she bit her lip as she listened to the options. After what seemed an eternity, she got a live person on the line. "Hello, my name is Erin McClellan. I'm a friend of Jack Langston's, who is a patient of Dr. Carmichael's."

"Do you have Mr. Langston's health-record number?"

"This is a bit of an emergency. Mr. Langston isn't well." She pawed through the contents of his wallet she'd left sprawled across his dresser until she found what looked like an insurance card.

"Try this." She read the number to the woman. "He's really not at all well—"

"One moment, please, while I pull up his record."

"Would it be possible to speak with Dr. Carmichael?"

"Dr. Carmichael is with a patient. What are Mr. Langston's symptoms?"

"He's in pain. I don't know what's wrong. It's his heart."

"Is he conscious?"

She glanced at him. "I think so."

"Miss, if there's a chance that he's having a heart attack, you need to hang up and dial nine-one-one for emergency assistance."

"Oh, God, of course. I'll do that." She hung up and dialed nine-one-one.

Stupid. Stupid. Why had she wasted time calling the doctor?

"Nine-one-one."

She gripped the phone. "Hi, I need help. I think my friend may be having a heart attack."

"Okay, stay calm. Let me verify the address and we'll get a unit out to you right away."

She verified the address, then answered a number of questions, all while the clock ticked away the minutes. Precious minutes that she'd wasted by not calling nine-one-one immediately, by not calling Jack when she'd gotten his message.

"Is he conscious?"

"Yes."

"Is he having pain anywhere else besides his chest?"

"Jack, does it hurt anywhere else?"

He shook his head.

"No, just his chest."

"Any other symptoms? Nausea, sweating, shortness of breath?"

"Jack, any nausea, sweating or shortness of breath?"

Again he shook his head.

"No."

"How long has he been having the pain?"

"I'm not sure. Here, I think he can talk to you." She held the phone to Jack's ear.

He scooted to more of a sitting position. "Hello… off and on since…last night, but it's gotten really bad just in the last ten minutes…or so."

He nodded and answered a few more short questions, his words halting. Then he thanked the operator and hung up. He met her gaze and gave her hand a squeeze. "Thanks, baby. They're dispatching a unit. It should be here in the next fifteen minutes. I'm sorry you're having to deal with this. Thought I'd be okay."

"*You're* sorry?" Her throat burned. "*I'm* sorry. I'm sorry I didn't call you back yesterday. I'm sorry you're having this pain. What can I do?"

"Hold me."

It didn't seem enough, not nearly enough, but she held him. He turned to her. "We…should talk."

"Later. I promise. You save your strength for now. I'm not going anywhere. I'll be around to talk all you want after this."

That seemed to satisfy him for the moment. He closed his eyes, and the quiet of the house settled over them. She soothed her hand over his chest and wished more than ever that she possessed some kind of healing power.

What she wouldn't do for this man.

At long last the doorbell rang. She eased herself from him, careful not to jostle him. Then she ran to the door, but it wasn't the paramedics. Jack's friend Amanda stood on his front step.

"Amanda."

"Hi. Erin, right? I thought you two split up."

"This isn't a good time. Jack isn't well."

A siren sounded in the distance.

Amanda frowned. "Where is he?"

The siren grew louder and an ambulance turned onto the street. Erin sighed in relief. "Thank God."

She left the door open and hurried back to the bedroom, Amanda on her heels. "What happened?" Amanda asked.

"I don't know. I came here a short while ago and found him like this. He's having chest pain."

"Oh, Jack." Amanda placed her hand on his forehead. "This wasn't supposed to happen, buddy."

"The paramedics are here," Erin said as the siren stopped and doors slammed in the driveway. She hurried out to find two uniformed paramedics carrying in a stretcher. "This way."

She stepped back as the paramedics took over.

Moments later she stood outside the ambulance with Amanda as they loaded Jack into the vehicle. She turned to Amanda. "Do you know how to contact his family?"

"He's not going to want them to know."

"Why not? He's close to his family. I know that much."

"Right, but what you may not know is that yesterday was D-day at the Langston's. That's short for Death Day. They have two of them every year. One to mark the day Jack's father died of a heart attack and one to mark the day his sister died. That was yesterday's. Seems they have a bad heart valve that runs in their family. Jack's grandfather had the same problem and died in his late thirties from it. Stacey, Jack's younger sister, was just sixteen when she started having problems. They did open-heart, but she didn't make it."

Erin stared at her, stunned. "I had no idea."

"Oh, yeah. And he's been having difficulties for the past six months or so, but he hasn't breathed a word to the rest of his family. He figures they've had enough grief."

"Oh, my God. This is going to devastate them."

"No shit. He's not going to have much choice now."

"About what?"

"About whether or not to have the same surgery that killed his sister."

Fear welled up inside Erin. "We don't know that'll happen. There's no use in panicking until we know what's happening. This might not even be a heart attack."

"Well, I'm going to call his mother. I've met her a few times. Better the news come from me than a stranger."

A stranger. Erin stood rooted to the driveway as Amanda headed back into Jack's condo. That's what she was. She'd hardly known Jack for a week and so much had happened in that time. It had been one hot, intense, out-of-control week, and now this. He had a whole life history that she knew nothing about. He'd been sick way before he met her.

What if sleeping with her had worsened his condition—had brought on a heart attack?

With a heavy heart she dragged herself inside to retrieve her things. Amanda spoke soothingly into the phone. Erin turned from her, her gut clenched.

Where were her keys? She had to get to the hospital. She might be a stranger to his family, but she was no stranger to Jack. And she had to be there for him, no matter what.

ALL HOSPITALS HAD THAT sterile, cold feeling. No amount of bright colors or homey curtains could change that. Erin hugged her arms to her chest and waited patiently while a man and woman spoke to the attendant behind the counter at the emergency check-in.

Fiberglass chairs hugged the walls and sat in joined rows inside the waiting area surrounded by mauve-colored walls. Half a dozen people or more sat in small groupings, murmuring in soft conversations. One young boy cried and a dark-haired woman comforted him.

The couple moved off, clipboard in hand, and Erin stepped up to the window. "Hi. A friend of mine was just brought in by ambulance. Would it be possible for me to see him?"

"What's your friend's name?"

"Jack Langston."

The woman flipped through some pages on a clipboard. "I don't have him. Let me see if he's been entered into the system yet."

"Thank you."

Amanda arrived, moving beside her at the counter. "How is he?"

"She's checking to see if he's in the system."

The woman turned from her computer screen. "I'm sorry. He hasn't been entered yet. Let me call over and make sure he's here."

"Thank you." Erin turned to Amanda. "You spoke with his mother?"

"They're on the way."

Erin nodded, feeling bereft. She didn't even know who "they" were.

The attendant hung up the phone and turned to them. "Jack Langston has just been admitted. The doctor is looking at him now. It's going to be a little while. You might as well have a seat."

"Okay, should we just check back here?" Erin asked. "He has family on the way."

"After the doctor looks at him, he'll tell the family members what his condition is, but he can't release any specific information."

Amanda smirked. "HIPPA regulations."

"Exactly. We can't tell you anything unless Mr. Langston signs a paper saying we can. You ladies can wait if you'd like."

"Thank you."

They moved off to two chairs in a corner of the waiting area. Amanda held her purse in her lap. "I was afraid something like this was going to happen. I just hoped it wouldn't."

"How long have you known Jack?"

"About five years. We met on the beach." She shook her head. "You don't have to worry. We've never been anything but friends."

"So what else don't I know about him?" Erin asked.

"Let's see…. He's a great cook. Did you know that?"

"Yes. He made meat loaf." She cleared her throat. "I guess we never actually ate it, though. But it smelled heavenly."

"He was pretty young when his father died. He became man of the house then. He took over pretty much everything, not just the cooking. I don't know how his family would have made it without him. They still struggle to manage. He's been trying to wean them, but I'm not sure how that's going. Jack has a hard time letting people down, even if it's in his best interest."

"He never mentioned any of that. He told me he got tired of eating out. He never really told me much about his family, other than that they were important to him."

"They are. He visits fairly often. His mother still lives in the house he grew up in. Her sister lives with her. It's a big house. The two of them rattle around in it. I visited with Jack over the holidays last year. His brother Bobby lives nearby. He keeps a closer watch, but he reports everything to Jack."

"They sound like wonderful people." Erin paused, then asked, "Why do you think he didn't tell me about his heart condition?"

"I don't think he's told anyone but me. We power walk the beach together. It became apparent that he was having trouble. He didn't want his family to know for obvious reasons. He said they'd just worry, and since there wasn't anything they could do, he didn't want to burden them."

"I understand that, but I wish he'd confided in me. I know I haven't known him for very long, but I thought we were closer." She had certainly felt closer to Jack than she'd ever felt to anyone else.

"Oh, he's nuts about you, let me assure you. I saw him the other day after you'd dumped him. He was a mess. I've never seen him so distraught."

"I don't know what to say."

"Erin, look, I'm not sure what made you go to see him today and I know you care about him and he cares about you, but I think the best thing you can do for Jack is to stay away from him."

"Oh." Erin straightened. "I was kind of thinking the same thing myself, but why do you think so?"

"I don't know that you're what he needs right now. We're not even going to contemplate his not making it. Once he gets over this, he's going to need lots of rest and relaxation. I get the idea the two of you haven't exactly been relaxing."

Warmth filled Erin's cheeks. "We have a very strong chemistry between us. We both tend to get a little…out of control."

"There you go. Well, I'm guessing he's not going to be up to any of that for a while. That and I don't know what you did to him, but he has been sick as a dog since he met you. It isn't what I thought would happen at all."

"Excuse me?"

Amanda's eyes widened. "I mean, I figured when he met someone new it would energize him. You know, give him a new outlook."

"So he was better before we met?"

"He had the heart stuff—tightening in his chest, fatigue, occasional dizziness—but none of that other stomach stuff he's had going on."

"I was afraid of that."

"Amanda." A pretty woman with Jack's coloring rushed up to them, followed by another woman and a young man. "How is he? Can we see him?"

Amanda rose and Erin followed suit, while Amanda made the introductions. "Grace Langston, this is Erin McClellan, another friend of Jack's. She's the one who found him. The doctor is with him now. Hopefully we'll know something soon."

"But what happened?" Grace asked. "We saw him Saturday night and he seemed fine."

Amanda took her hand. "I'm so sorry you've had to find out like this. He hasn't been well for a while. He didn't want to worry you. That's why he didn't tell you."

"So he's seen a cardiologist and it's a congenital defect?" Grace asked.

"He said that it's the same as with his father and sister."

"And his grandfather," the second woman added.

Grace closed her eyes. "My poor Jack. He should have told us. What did his doctor say? Did he recommend surgery?"

"He did, but after what happened with Stacey, Jack was looking into alternative treatments," Amanda explained.

"What kind of alternative treatments?" Grace asked. "You can't treat something like that with herbs and diet."

"No, but he was looking at different types of energy work." Amanda's gaze flickered over Erin. "Like reiki and acupuncture."

A feeling of foreboding settled over Erin. Good God, what was Amanda saying? Surely Jack hadn't known about her family when he'd walked into her shop that day?

"For Pete's sake." Grace seemed almost ready to collapse.

Amanda motioned to the chairs. "Why don't you have a seat?"

Jack's mother extended her hand to Erin. "Please call me Grace, both of you girls. Erin, this is my sister, Rose, and my son, Bobby."

Erin shook hands with Rose and Bobby, who

looked like a younger version of Jack. Bobby smiled. "You're the one redoing his place, aren't you?"

"Yes. We signed a contract just last week." Last week. It seemed an eternity ago.

Grace cocked her head. "Oh, yes, the girl he mentioned at dinner. You must be very special to him, dear. Jack never mentions his girlfriends."

"Why don't we all sit down?" Rose suggested. "Bobby, maybe you can find us some coffee or something. Don't all hospitals have cafeterias or those little vending machines?"

"I'm on it, Aunt Rose. What can I get for everybody?"

Rose and Amanda gave their orders, while Grace and Erin declined. Then Amanda left with Bobby to find the coffee. Grace turned to Erin. "So how long have you known my son?"

"About a little over a week, though it seems much longer."

"Just like you and Stan," Rose said to Grace. "The two of them had a whirlwind courtship. They were married within a month after meeting each other. I thought they were insane. Told them it would never work."

Grace smiled a sad, tired smile. "Well, she was wrong. I was all of twenty when we married and we were together for fourteen glorious years. I've no doubt we'd be married still if Stan was with us."

Grace's pain drew Erin and she reached for her, placing her hand on the older woman's. "He's going to be all right."

Jack's mother nodded. "We have to believe that, don't we?"

"Yes. I'm so sorry you're going through this. Whatever happens, please don't be upset with Jack for not telling you."

"Oh, of course not. He was trying to take care of me, just like he always has." Her gaze warmed and she placed her other hand on top of Erin's. "I'm not sure what you are to him, but I have a wonderful feeling about you. I'm so glad you're in his life and you can be here for him right now."

"To be honest, I'm not sure what I am to him either, but I promised him while we were waiting for the ambulance that I'm not going anywhere," Erin said.

The doors that led to the care units swung open and a nurse called the name Langston. Erin waved her over. The nurse stopped in front of them. "Are you Jack Langston's family?"

"I'm his mother and this is his aunt and this young lady is a very good friend of his. How is my son?"

"He's stable, but we're keeping him for observation. You can see him two at a time. I'll take you back."

"You two go," Erin said to Grace and Rose. "I can wait."

Grace nodded and gave her hand one last squeeze before she stood to follow the nurse.

13

THE DOOR TO THE HOSPITAL room scraped and Jack opened his eyes. His mother and aunt moved beside his bed. He smiled and tried to sit up but got tangled in the IV and wires connected to his chest. "There are my two favorite sweethearts."

His mother sank into the chair beside the bed. She smoothed his hair from his forehead. "Look at you, all plugged in."

"Doctors. They have to run all their tests. How are you doing?"

Her eyes widened. "Do you hear that, Rose? He asks how am *I* doing? You're always looking after me, aren't you, Jack? I'm hanging in here, dear. The question is how are *you?*"

"Tired. Having people wait on you isn't all it's cracked up to be."

Rose leaned on the bed rail. "We understand why you didn't tell us you were having trouble, but what did the doctor say?"

He blew out a slow breath. God, he was exhausted. "Seems I had just a very small…minor…heart attack, but I'm okay for now."

"For now." Grace exchanged a worried look with her sister. "And what about surgery, Jack? Did you talk to the doctor about that?"

"The E.R. doctor actually got my regular cardiologist on the phone. The two of them talked. Dr. Carmichael had already recommended that I have the surgery months ago. I'm going to stay here overnight for observation, then he's going to work me in tomorrow so we can talk about options."

"What options? You have to have the surgery," Grace said.

He gave her hand a squeeze. "Don't worry, Mom. I promise I'll take care of this. I see the surgery as a last resort."

"Sweetie, what happened to Stacey doesn't have to happen to you. That was a fluke, a bad reaction to the anesthesia or something. Who knows? They do valve repairs all the time. Every surgery has its risks, but in this day and age the odds are in your favor."

He fisted his hands at the worry in their eyes. How could he have let them down like this? "I do understand that. I just want to make sure that I've exhausted all alternatives before I let them cut me open."

"What alternatives? What is this about you looking into—what was it?" Grace asked Rose.

"Energy work. Acupuncture."

"Acupuncture. Thank you. How is that supposed to help? What did you do? Did you let some quack doctor stick needles in your chest?"

"He stuck them all over my body, actually. Very strange experience, not nearly as bad as I anticipated. The needles are really sharp. You can barely feel them."

"Jack, that's nonsense. You can't be serious about any of that," his mother said.

"Amanda's been telling you a little too much." A sense of unease gripped him. "Where's Erin? Did she come?"

"She's in the waiting room. She's a wonderful girl, Jack. She's very worried about you. Surely she doesn't support you in this quest for…alternative treatments."

"She didn't know I was defective."

Rose patted his leg. "You're not defective, pet. Your valve's defective. That's not quite the same."

"Thank you, Aunt Rose."

"Bobby and Amanda are both here, too, but the nurse said you could only see two of us at a time."

"I would really like to see Erin, if you two don't mind."

"Not at all." His mother leaned over him and

kissed his forehead. "I love you, my big, sweet boy. You get yourself better. Please call me later and let me know how you're doing."

"I will. 'Bye, Aunt Rose. Don't forget to send Erin back."

He closed his eyes again as they left, the weariness taking him. He could sleep for a week after this. Then maybe he'd wake up to find it had all been a bad dream and he was as healthy and hearty as ever. All a dream except the part about Erin, of course.

"Jack?" Her soft voice drifted to him as if from the dream.

He opened his eyes, his lids seeming to weigh two tons each. Erin stood beside his bed, her face drawn with worry, her green eyes watery. He reached for her and pulled her toward him, but the damn bed rail got in the way. He let go of her to wrestle with the thing and she helped him to lower it.

Then she sat beside him. "Oh, Jack, you scared the hell out of me. Your mom said that you had a heart attack."

"Just a teeny-tiny one." He pinched his fingers together to show her. If this was how he felt after a minor heart attack, what would happen when the real thing came along?

"Why didn't you tell me?"

He took her hand, savoring the warmth that

flowed into him. "You really do have magic, you know. I can feel it now. Your touch is golden."

"What if my touch put you here?" Tears glistened on her cheeks.

"Oh, baby, is that what you think?" He moved his arm to hold her, but his IV got in the way again. "If anything, you probably kept this from happening sooner."

"I don't think so."

"Erin, listen, I understand how you feel, but you have to understand that I don't care if being with you made me a little queasy afterward. It was well worth it. It always passed, and I swear to you when the nausea was over I felt energized and vibrant. Other than making love to you, there isn't a better feeling."

"Jack—"

"I'd been having symptoms—tightening in my chest, shortness of breath, sometimes I'd get dizzy and feel like I was going to fall over and I didn't have any energy. That all stopped the moment I met you." He stroked her hand. "I don't care what you say. You have magic and I know it's helped me."

"You knew, didn't you?"

The hurt in her voice drew his gaze to her, tightened his throat. "I knew what?"

"You knew about my family. You came to my design studio looking for me that day not because you wanted to have your house redone. You came look-ing for a sexual healer, didn't you?"

He closed his eyes as his world crashed down around him. "Yes."

She didn't respond. He glanced at her, remorse choking him. She sat with her head down, her shoul-ders shaking with silent tears.

"Baby, don't cry. I'm so sorry. I should have told you. I just... I didn't want to lose you."

"Why?" She looked up and tears streaked down her face.

She was the most beautiful woman he'd ever seen. Her tears brightened the green of her eyes, and it wrenched his gut to see the misery he'd caused her.

He struggled with the IV and gripped her arms. "Please, Erin, don't be upset with me. I was desper-ate enough to seek you out and hope you might be able to help me. I didn't have a plan when I walked in your door. I didn't know how these things worked—if we'd strike up some kind of business deal.

"You were so upset at just the mention of your family, and when I realized that you were in denial about being a sexual healer, I knew I'd made a mis-take," he said. "But it was already too late for me to walk away. From the minute I laid eyes on you I knew I had to make you mine, not just for a quickie miracle lay but for however long it might last. You completely captivated me with just one touch. I want to be with you. We don't have to be lovers if that upsets you, but please…don't leave me. I need you."

Tears continued to stream down her face. "I'm so sorry. I can't be what you want. I can't give you what you need."

"Erin, no—"

"I know I said I'd be here, but I'm afraid if I stay I'll only cause you more misery."

"No, you won't." His throat burned. The room blurred.

She rose from the bed. "Goodbye, Jack."

"Erin, wait." He clenched his fists as the door closed behind her.

"ERIN? OH, MY GOODNESS, what is it?" Aunt Sophie stepped back from the door.

Erin moved, her legs numb. She collapsed in the closest chair, one of the big overstuffed ones in her aunt's living room. Thomas and Maggie turned to her from their place on the couch. Thomas clicked the remote, and the TV they'd been watching silenced.

"What's happened, girl?" he asked.

Erin's gaze swept across their worried faces. "I'm a fraud. A fake. I don't deserve the name McClellan."

Maggie moved beside her, perching on the cushion, while Thomas and Aunt Sophie hovered nearby.

Maggie smoothed her hand on Erin's knee. "Now take a deep breath and tell us what's happened."

"I'm not a sexual healer." She hiccuped and a tear rolled down her cheek. "I'm the opposite of that. I'm a sexual antihealer. That's it. I'm the antihealer."

"Why would you think such a thing?" Sophie asked. "It can't be."

"I make men sick. All this time everyone thought I was heartbroken over my breakup with Ryan, I was just mortified. The man puked his guts out for four days in my bedroom. He was too sick to leave. And he wasn't the first. But by then I couldn't deny it anymore. It was me. No freak coincidence. No stomach bug." She looked at all of them through the tears in her eyes. "Just me. I sleep with a guy and it makes him positively ill."

"You don't say?" Aunt Sophie glanced at Maggie. "Have you heard of this before?"

"No, but these girls are taking the gift to a whole new level."

"Gift? Aren't you listening? I don't have the gift. I'm some freak of the genetic pool. Some sick joke in the McClellan family."

"No, you're not." Maggie handed her a handkerchief from Thomas. "Now exactly what happens to these men? What are the symptoms?"

"Mostly they throw up. There's sweating and

stomach cramps and all that other gastrointestinal stuff. It's horrible. I couldn't believe it the first couple of times, but believe me, there's no doubt about it. I make men sick." Fresh tears coursed down her cheeks. "What the hell kind of gift is that?"

"I don't know, Sophie, what do you think? Sounds like some kind of purging to me," Maggie said.

"Yes, I think you're right. Erin, after they get sick, what happens?"

"What do you mean what happens? Either they leave or I leave. It's a little hard to carry on a relationship if your boyfriend ralphs every time you…you know."

"So that's why you always dump them so fast." Maggie pursed her lips.

Thomas shook his head. "Poor bastards."

"Thomas, that's not helpful." Sophie turned toward the kitchen. "We need some honey cakes and tea. Let me see…I think I know the perfect blend."

"I know she means well, but how is tea going to help?" Erin asked her mother.

"Oh, your aunt's teas always help. It isn't just the herbs, you know. Sophie has another magic all her own."

Thomas nodded. "Amen."

Erin stared at both of them. "My life is ruined. I have likely put a man in the hospital and all you can suggest is that I drink tea?"

"What man? What hospital?" Maggie asked.

"This new guy I've been seeing. Jack. I really like him. *Really* like him. I thought at first that he was different. I didn't mean to sleep with him. When I realized I was Typhoid Mary, I swore off men. I'd rather be celibate than keep doing that to them.

"But with Jack, I don't know…I couldn't help myself. I lost control. We both did, especially that first time, and then it didn't seem like he was getting sick. I didn't find out until later that he had, but for some reason he hadn't told me," Erin explained.

"Anyway, he has a bad heart." Erin wiped her nose. "Something he was born with. His grandfather and his father and his younger sister all had the same thing. His grandfather and father both died at an early age because of it. And his sister had surgery when she was just sixteen to fix it, but she died on the operating table.

"It's just horrible, and I didn't know any of this, but when I found out he was getting sick I broke things off with him. Then I went to see him, really I went to measure his place for the redesign. I didn't think he was home because he hadn't answered the phone, and I found him in his bed."

Her throat burned with the memory. "He had a heart attack. I called nine-one-one. I just left the hospital. I broke things off with him for good."

"Oh, my God, angel. Come here." Maggie opened her arms and Erin fell into them. She cried until she couldn't cry anymore.

When at last she pulled back, Aunt Sophie had arrived with the tea tray and a plate of honey cakes. She smiled warmly at Erin, her eyes filled with compassion. "Good thing I bake these regularly."

"Here." Maggie handed Erin a cup of hot tea.

Erin breathed in the steam, then took a tentative sip. Whatever her aunt had brewed, it warmed her from the inside out. She blew on the hot liquid, then drank some more, while Maggie retold her sad tale to Aunt Sophie.

Aunt Sophie shook her head. "Oh, sugar, you know you didn't have anything to do with his heart attack."

"No," Maggie agreed. "He had issues with his heart long before you met him. And a heart attack doesn't fall along the same lines as the other symptoms you've described. No, the more I think about it, the more I believe you have the gift of purging. I'll bet if we were to look up any of your young men we would find them hale and hearty and a world better for having made your acquaintance."

Maybe it was the tea, but a small ray of hope opened over Erin. She sniffed. "Really? You think that maybe it isn't a bad thing?"

Her mother cocked her head. "We can't always answer the whys or hows, but the one thing I can promise you is that the gift has always been used to heal. It seems to have manifested in quite an unusual way with you, but it sounds like the gift to me."

"Definitely," her aunt agreed. "Why don't you call one of your young men and see what happens?"

"You're kidding. Call some guy I dumped or who dumped me because every time after we slept together he ended up stuck in the bathroom, hugging the toilet?"

"That's right." Sophie handed her the phone. "Do you have any of their numbers?"

Erin stared at the phone. Call them? "No. I don't have any of their numbers. I was never with anyone long enough to memorize them."

"Or program them into your cell phone?" Thomas asked.

"No, I never programmed any of them into my cell phone."

"But you have their numbers somewhere at home?"

She paused, considering. "Yes. I have one or two of their numbers."

"Good, then you'll call them and let us know what happens." Aunt Sophie raised her teacup with a satisfied nod.

Erin stared at her a long moment. "I don't know. It would be weird to call out of the blue like that."

"But I'll bet that they'll be thrilled to hear from you," Maggie said.

"I don't think so," Erin said, unease filling her.

"You should try, love." Maggie stirred sugar into her tea. "How else will you know if you were right to break up with Jack? What if being with you made him stronger, so he could withstand the heart attack? What if it would have been much worse had you not been with him? What if being with you now is his best shot at fully recovering? You just can't know—" Maggie gave her a pointed look "—unless you ask."

The hope in Erin's heart stirred. She looked again from her mother to her aunt, then to Thomas, who nodded reassuringly. Then she swallowed. "Okay, I'll make a few calls."

14

ERIN'S PULSE THRUMMED as she stared at the number in her cell phone. Okay, maybe she'd lied a little the other night. She had programmed at least one of her ex-lovers into her cell phone.

While Trent had been working with her, she'd talked to him almost every day. She hadn't been about to call him right there in front of everyone, though. Some things were meant to be done in private.

She flexed her hands and took a deep breath. She had to do this. Maggie's questions burned through her.

How else will you know if you were right to break up with Jack? You just can't know unless you ask.

"Okay, here goes nothing." She pushed the call button on her phone.

The display showed her phone dialing Trent's number. With her breath held and her eyes closed she pressed the phone to her ear. He picked up before the third ring. "Erin?"

"Trent. Hi. I'll bet you're surprised to hear from me."

"Oh, my God. Can you hold on just a sec and let me get rid of this other call?"

"Sure."

"Okay. I'll be right back. Don't go anywhere."

"I won't." She let out her breath when he clicked over but had barely had time to refill her lungs before he was back.

"I can't believe it's you. I am so excited you called," he said.

"You are?"

"You bet. I've been meaning to call you, but I've been so caught up in everything."

"You have? What's been going on with you?"

"What hasn't been going on with me? New job, new look, I feel like I'm finally making something of myself. I hate that I left the way I did, Erin, honestly. You must think I'm the slime of the earth for not calling.

"I never meant to leave you hanging like that," he said. "After I left you that day, I spent three days feeling like I was dying. It was the worst intestinal bug I'd ever had. But in some way it was the best thing that ever happened to me.

"Somehow afterward I felt transformed. I woke up on that last day and I felt like a new man—like I had a whole new lease on life. I don't know how exactly, but I think it had something to do with the time I spent with you. That's because that's how you made me feel when we were together that night.

"That one encounter with you was the most uplifting event of my life. That's the honest truth," he said. "Then I had to blow it all by getting sick, but I think it helped me. Got me to get rid of a bunch of extra stuff I had in me or something." He paused.

"I can't explain it, but you've turned my life around. I can never repay you. I started to call you so many times, but I guess I was a little in awe of you after that and, well, the way I left… It was all a little humbling. Truth was, I didn't think I could face you or explain myself coherently. And here you are calling me and I can't seem to shut myself up."

She smiled, more than a little stunned herself. "I'm glad you told me all that. I'm so happy to hear that you're doing well. I can't say that I had anything to do with it, but sounds like you're in a happy place."

"I am and it *was* because of you. I'm convinced of that. I mentioned it to Josh and he said it was the same for him with Tess. You girls have got some kind of gift, you know."

"So I've been told."

"What can I do for you? Do you need help with your design business? I've gotten myself pretty wrapped up in a major project, but I'll do anything for you."

"No, I'm good. I just wanted to say hi and see how you were doing," she said.

"I'm so glad you called. You doing okay?"

"Oh, sure. I'm great. You take care, Trent, and thanks for sharing all that with me."

He bid her an enthusiastic goodbye, then she pushed the disconnect button, a sense of wonder filling her. Were her mother and Aunt Sophie right? Did she really have the gift? Could it be that just maybe she was what Jack needed after all?

She raced to her nightstand to find her address book and all the scraps of paper she'd stuffed into it bearing numbers she'd meant to one day record in the pages. After several minutes of searching, she found Ryan's number.

Without hesitating she pressed it into the keypad on her phone, but to her disappointment his voice mail picked up. "Hi, Ryan, this is Erin McClellan. I know it's been a while, but I thought I'd check to see how you're doing. Give me a call sometime."

She left her number, just in case, then disconnected. "Let's see, who else?"

She flipped through her address book again. She couldn't go on just one positive response. She had to talk to someone else. If she found more reactions like Trent's, then maybe she didn't need to be on her own.

She'd have a good reason to go back to Jack.

JACK SIPPED HIS COFFEE and stared out the window of his childhood bedroom. The ache in his chest was of a different sort these days. This ache could only be the pain of a broken heart.

"You ready, bro?" Bobby popped his head through the doorway.

Jack glanced around. "Just need my shoes."

"Here, I've got them." Bobby whisked them out of the closet and at Jack's feet before Jack could work up the energy to push himself off the bed.

Funny how quickly the tables had turned. Since his little visit to the hospital, his family couldn't do enough for him. He gritted his teeth. He should be grateful, but he hated that his family's sudden ability to take care of themselves came because he'd been disabled.

"Thanks." With a slowness that didn't have anything to do with his recent illness Jack slipped on his shoes.

He was stalling. Why should he hurry? What man would rush to have his chest sliced open?

"I'll warm up the car. You got it okay?" Bobby asked.

"Sure, Bobby, I'm fine. I'm coming. I'm not an invalid. I can drag my fat ass to the car on my own."

"Okay. I'll tell Mom we're going then."

Jack nodded, feeling like a jerk. His brother hadn't deserved his sarcasm. None of them had deserved his sour mood over the past few days, but he hated this weakness. And since Erin had walked out on him the last time, an oppressive gloom had settled over him.

He closed his eyes and pushed himself up from the bed. Maybe he should call her to make sure she was all right after all that drama at the hospital and to tell her about the surgery. Maybe if she knew he was taking care of his little problem, she might consider coming back to him.

I'm afraid if I stay I'll only cause you more misery.

Silly woman. Didn't she know all he was without her was miserable? He dug his cell phone from his pocket. He scrolled through his contacts to her name, then pressed the call button.

She answered on the second ring, her voice breathless. "Ryan?"

"No. This is Jack."

"Oh, Jack, hi. How are you?" she asked. "I called the hospital to check your condition, but they said you'd been released."

"They just kept me overnight."

"So are you feeling any better?"

"No, I'm miserable. I miss you like hell, Erin. Please come back to me. I know I'm no prize package with my defect and all, but I'm getting that taken care of. I need you. I want you. I don't care if I puke buckets a day. It's all worth it. I'd rather spend a day being sick with you than spend another minute in this hell without you. There, I'm groveling, but that's it. I'm a man with no strength. I have no dignity left. I have nothing if I don't have you. And who the hell is Ryan?"

Silence buzzed across the line and he wanted to kick himself for running on. She'd probably hung up. Then a soft sob sounded from her end.

"Hell, baby, I didn't mean to make you cry," he said.

"I'm sorry, Jack. I'm not ready to see you. I want to, really I do, but I can't risk it yet."

"Yet? That sounds hopeful."

"What do you mean you're taking care of it? Are you having the surgery?"

"I'm headed out the door right now."

His mother stepped into his room. "Jack, we're going to be late."

He motioned to her to wait a minute. "I have to go, Erin. Promise you'll come see me."

"Jack…I'll be thinking about you and sending you prayers and good wishes."

"Great. Thanks." His throat tightened. Prayers and good wishes. He should count his blessings.

"Jack." His mother motioned for him to come.

He closed his eyes. "Baby, I—I'll call you later."

He hung up before he could hear her response or make a further fool of himself. She'd already said it all. She wasn't ready to see him.

Well, hell, they could have his heart now. They might as well cut it out altogether and rid him of it once and for all. A lot of damn good it was doing him.

He gritted his teeth and headed down the stairs, his mother on his heels. She meant well, but Erin was the only one he wanted at that moment. If only he could see her. He could get through this with just one hug, one touch or even a smile from the woman he loved.

ERIN CLOSED HER EYES and leaned back in her office chair. Her whole body ached. She'd hardly slept in days and Jack's words continued to haunt her, distracting her from her work at hand.

I'd rather spend a day being sick with you than spend another minute in this hell without you.

If only she could be sure she wouldn't cause him any harm, she'd drop everything to rush to his side. Her stomach tightened at the thought of him facing the surgery. At least he had his family with him.

Stacey, Jack's younger sister, was just sixteen when she started having problems. They did open-heart, but she didn't make it.

A shiver of fear raced through Erin. What would she do if he didn't make it?

What if being with you now is his best shot at fully recovering?

She pushed back her chair. What if he really needed her? Should she go to the hospital? "I'm damned if I do and damned if I don't."

Her frustration building, she grabbed her purse, then headed out the door. She at least had to find out how he was doing. She didn't have to see him, but she could go to the hospital and wait for news along with the rest of them.

A cool gust hit her as she exited the building. A man waved to her as she crossed the street to her car. He moved nearer and a rush of recognition hit her. "Ryan!"

Smiling broadly, he rushed up to her, his eyes shining, the perfect picture of health. "Erin McClellan, you are a sight for sore eyes."

"I could say the same for you." She threw her arms around him and hugged him tight.

A sound of satisfaction rose from him and he held her close for a long moment before she pulled back smiling. His entire demeanor shone. Surely he'd have good news to report, as well, then she'd know it would probably be safe to visit Jack. "You look a whole lot better than the last time I saw you."

He groaned and clutched his stomach. "The agony, the humiliation. What a way to impress a woman."

"You didn't need to impress me. You had already done that."

"You certainly impressed the hell out of me. I've never experienced anything like that. I felt like I'd hit the lottery when I got your message.

"I would have called you sooner, but I've been out of town and didn't check voice mail until I got back this morning," he explained. "I was going to call you back, but I was right around the corner, so I figured I'd just pop over. Looks like I just caught you."

"You did. I'm headed to the hospital to see a friend who's having surgery. I called you to see how you're doing."

"Really?" His eyes brightened. "After what happened, I didn't think you'd ever want anything to do with me. When I left your place that day I felt like a dog running off with my tail between my legs.

"Man, it was bad. I have never been sick like that," he said. "Then I woke up that next morning and I had broken this major sweat and the puking and all that was gone like it had never happened.

"I felt…invincible. For days it was like I kept reliving how it was when we were, you know, getting it on. Really strange, but I couldn't get you out of my mind and I felt like I was reborn or something. I sound like the biggest ass, but, Erin, that whole experience with you, even though those were some of the most wretched days of my life, it was also the coolest, the most spiritual time." He laughed.

"Okay, I'm talking like a geek, but it's the honest-to-God truth. And I wanted to call you months ago, but then I met this girl. We're actually talking about hitching up. It's incredible. I've never felt better about my life. She's an angel, and I know this is going to sound strange, but I could never have gotten with her if I hadn't been with you first and gone through all that.

"Sounds bizarre and I guess it is, but there you are. That's how I've been."

"I'm so glad to hear everything is going so well for you, Ryan. Thanks. I needed to hear that."

He shrugged. "Is that all you need? I feel so indebted to you. If there's anything else I can do for you, you call me and I'm here."

"Thank you." She went up on tiptoe and kissed his cheek. "You've made my day."

He touched his cheek, his eyes wide. "You've got the magic. It's all in your touch."

She cocked her head and, for the first time in ages, laughter bubbled up inside her.

15

COMFORT, WARMTH AND LIGHT. Jack drifted in a place of peace. Something—a feeling—tugged at him, and he tried to focus on it, but it broke apart and dissipated like fog. He drifted again and the feeling—longing— pulled at him. He moved away from it, back into the peaceful oblivion of light and air, but the longing found him and filled him. Darkness surrounded him.

Need and want, aching want. He reached into the ether to fill the emptiness, reached for someone—a woman who wasn't there. The memory of her shimmered before him, her form just beyond his grasp, her face and name eluding him. The ache became despair.

Grief welled up inside him, consuming him in its intensity. Pain radiated from his chest outward in a deep, dull ache that penetrated beyond his body, his mind, into his essence. He sought the blessed oblivion, but like the woman, it escaped him, and his thoughts took form. He surfaced into glimpses of memory.

For an instant her image cleared before him, her

face radiant, her arms open to him. A sense of well-being flowed over him and her love, strong and powerful, filled him to overflowing.

He was complete.

Then she disappeared, and along with her, the peace and the love. He reached for her but touched only emptiness as the ache returned to his chest, pressing into him with an oppressive heaviness. Her face flashed before him one last time.

Erin.

"Jack? Honey, can you hear me? I think he's coming to. Did you see he moved?" A woman's voice, so familiar.

"He came out of the anesthesia okay earlier, but he's still pretty sedated, but he is coming around. His pulse is steady and holding. His blood pressure's not bad. Like I said, the surgery took a little longer than I'd anticipated, but overall he looks good. I'll be back to check on him in a few hours."

The doctor. That was his doctor. Dr…

"You want me to get you some coffee or something to drink?" a man's voice said, again hauntingly familiar.

"No, I'm fine, Bobby."

Bobby, his brother, and the woman was his mother. Jack struggled to open his eyes, but his eyelids had never felt this heavy. And he was so tired.

Erin.

He tried to say her name, but his mouth wouldn't move as the fog again closed in around him.

"ERIN, WHY DON'T YOU GO home and get some rest?" Jack's aunt Rose shuffled through a pile of magazines on a small side table in the hospital waiting room.

Erin yawned and looked at her watch. It was well past midnight. "I can't leave. I want to be here when he wakes up."

"I don't think that's going to be anytime tonight," Bobby said as he drew near. "He started to come around just a little while ago, but he never really woke up all the way. The nurse said he'd probably sleep through the night." He pursed his lips. "They're going to keep him in ICU for a while. Even if he did wake up, you wouldn't be able to see him."

Rose stood and stretched. "Come on, Erin, I'll walk you out. I know that sister of mine and she won't leave his side. I need a good night's sleep." She turned to Bobby. "Are you coming?"

"I'll hang out with Mom and Jack for a bit." He turned to Erin. "We'll call you tomorrow when he wakes up."

Rose pulled her car keys from her bag and glanced questioningly at Erin. She stood slowly, her muscles aching from sitting so long. "Please tell Jack I'll be waiting to hear from him," she said to Bobby.

"I will. I promise. I'm sure you'll be the first one he asks for."

Erin shivered as she reached her car and waved good-night to Rose. She glanced at the hospital and a sense of unease filled her. She slid into the driver's seat and gripped the wheel. Jack would be okay.

He had to be.

"YOU HAVEN'T SEEN HIM YET?" Nikki gazed at Tess, her eyes filled with concern.

They sat on Erin's bed. Her normal bed in her normal room in her pitifully normal apartment. After two days of pacing the length of her living room and jumping every time her phone rang, she'd broken down when Nikki called to check on her and begged her to come over.

"He's been in intensive care. Now it seems he's developed an infection. He started running a fever yesterday." Erin scrunched her pillow close to her chest. "I keep telling myself he'll be fine, but I can't eat. I can't sleep. I'm sick with worry."

"Have you talked to Mason? Maybe he can give Jack's cardiologist a call."

"I've been staying off the phone. Bobby promised he'd call if there was any change in Jack's condition." She rocked, still holding the pillow. "I just can't stand it. Another day of this and I think I might snap."

"I'll talk to Mason for you. Maybe he can write you a prescription for something to help you relax. You need to sleep, Erin. When Jack's out of ICU, he's going to need you."

"He was so weak when I last saw him. He needed me and I left him." Her throat burned. "I was so afraid I'd make him sick again. I couldn't risk it."

"No, of course you couldn't, but now you know you really have the gift. Eventually when he recovers enough, you'll be able to be with him again and you'll know that there's no better medicine."

Erin brushed a stray tear from her cheek. "I'd like to believe that."

"Even with all those testimonials you're not ready to embrace the McClellan in you?"

"You mean the gift." Erin shook her head. "It's not so easy after all this time. I might not be able to deny I have it anymore, but accepting it might take me some time."

She paused a long moment. "I don't know how I feel about how Jack sought me out for my gift and how he never said a word about it. It really hurts, you know?"

"But it's hard to blame him. Would you have done any different if you were him?"

"Maybe it's good that I can't see him right now," Erin said.

Nikki nodded. "It all takes getting used to. I wasn't all that thrilled when I learned about the gift. Your gift sends men running for the bathroom. Mine sent them running from my bed. I know how you feel. It took me a while to accept it, too."

"It sounds crazy, given all that and that I've known him for such a short time, but the one thing I can't deny is that I love him, Nikki. I love him with all my heart."

"Then he should pull through just fine. He already has the best medicine of all."

A SOFT RUSTLING SOUNDED in the darkness. Jack startled awake, straining to see in the dim light filtering through the window of his hospital room. The weight on his chest still pressed down on him, and the fatigue and fever plagued him. He squinted. A shape loomed from the shadows near the door.

"Bobby? Is that you?" he asked.

His brother moved into the patch of moonlight falling through the window. He motioned with his finger to his lips, then whispered, "I've smuggled you in a surprise. Thought this might boost your spirits."

Erin stepped from the shadows. She stood for a moment, her hands clasped over her chest. "Hi, Jack."

He turned his head, unease and regret filling him. "I'm a mess. I don't want you to see me like this."

"You look beautiful to me." She moved beside him. Her cool hand touched his cheek.

"I'll leave you two," Bobby said, then slipped into the shadows. The door scraped and light fell around the opening as he exited, then the shadows again covered them.

Erin moved toward the head of the bed. "Should I turn on a light?"

"No. I like the dark."

"Okay." The bed rail made a soft squealing sound, then her weight shifted the mattress as she sat beside him. "I've been so worried about you."

She had come to him. Where was the joy? The real-life woman of his dreams had come to him at long last, but the despair still yawned before him.

Her presence pained him. How could Bobby have brought her here when Jack was like this—half a man with no strength to even reach for her hand?

"I've been thinking about you," he said. "All this time I've had to lie here and stare at the ceiling. I've been so selfish. That day in your shop, I should have told you right away how I'd tracked you down and why. Amanda had some friend of a friend of a friend or something and he knew a guy who knew one of your sisters.

"She'd healed him. Some lung problem, I think it was. There one minute, gone the next," he said. "I couldn't believe such things existed. Sexual healing. What a concept."

He shook his head. "I'm some piece of work. I'm all busted up and broken inside. Have this bum valve. And what do I do? I decide to find myself a sexual healer to fix it for me.

"Only the healer I find doesn't want anything to do with the old family gift. Does that stop me? Of course not. I sleep with her anyway. I sleep with her a lot, like some animal that can't keep his dick in his pants. What kind of guy would do such a thing?"

"That isn't how it was."

"Wasn't it? How can you care? How can you worry about me after I used you the way I did? And where did it land me?" A hoarse laugh tore from his throat.

"Jack, don't. You're not yourself." Her voice trembled.

"How would you know? It's not like we had many deep conversations while we were in the middle of screwing each other's brains out. What do you really know about me? Not a whole hell of a lot."

He was tired, so tired and sick of himself. She shouldn't see him like this. He didn't deserve her. He never had. "I'm so sorry, Erin. I should have stayed the hell away from you."

"No, that's not true." Her hand again touched his face. The magic flowed from her almost instantly.

"Don't touch me." He jerked away. He didn't deserve her touch.

"You're burning up."

Of course he was. He was in hell. He shouldn't be here. Guilt consumed him. He should have died on that operating table.

The ache inside him grew, burning his throat, stinging his eyes. He turned from her as much as the damn IV and whatever other crap they had him hooked to would let him. His throat felt raw, his nerves on edge as if he might laugh or cry at any given moment.

He couldn't bear another minute with her beside him. "Go. Please leave me."

She hesitated, then her weight shifted. "Let me hold you."

"No, don't. Just leave me." What would drive her from him? "I feel sick, like I might vomit again."

"Should I get a nurse?" Distress filled her voice.

"Just…go. I don't want you here."

She was silent a long moment and when she spoke, her throat was tight, her words shaky as if she'd been crying. "Okay, I'll go, but please call me when you're ready to see me."

He didn't answer her, just lay there wrapped in misery. Her weight lifted off the bed. The bed rail made that faint squeal. A moment later the light appeared around the door.

Then all went dark and he was alone. Alone and wretched. It was all he deserved.

He shouldn't have been the one to survive.

HONEY CAKES AND TEA WERE Aunt Sophie's answer to every misery visited on mankind. Erin stared at the untouched plate her aunt had left on the patio table beside her. A chill passed through her. She zipped her sweat jacket closed.

Thanksgiving loomed just around the corner, but she could find little to be thankful for. Bobby's latest reports said Jack was improving. His fever had abated but still lingered. She shivered. The temperature had dipped into the fifties, not too cold compared to what the rest of the country was experiencing, but she hadn't been able to escape the cold that had filled her that night Bobby had snuck her into the ICU.

Just…go. I don't want you here.

She blinked back the tears that stood ready to blur her vision. She'd cried herself into a dreamless sleep that night, then woken feeling raw and exhausted. She'd been walking around in a daze ever since, ignoring work, letting her apartment go.

Her cell phone rang. She jumped as it vibrated in her pocket, then scrambled to answer it. "Erin McClellan."

"Erin, it's Bobby."

His voice held a heaviness that couldn't mean good news. "Bobby, what is it? How's Jack?"

"His fever broke the other day. They moved him to a regular room. His blood count looks good. The infection has cleared. His vital signs are all stable."

She let out her breath. "Thank God. Are they releasing him?"

"Sometime today. We're taking him to Mom's. She and Aunt Rose want to fuss over him while he recovers. I'll check on them regularly and I'll be only fifteen minutes away if they need me."

"That's great. I'm so glad he has all of you. When do you think I can see him?"

A long silence stretched across the line and her stomach tightened. Finally Bobby cleared his throat. "He doesn't want to see you."

"Oh." The cold pressed to her bones. "I see."

"He's not himself, Erin. He's…I don't know, it's like he's given up, like he doesn't want to be here anymore."

Fear laced Bobby's words. Aunt Sophie's backyard blurred. Erin's throat ached. She nodded, unable to speak.

"We're not sure what to do with him. His doctor has recommended counseling, but Jack refuses." Bobby said.

Oh, Jack. She closed her eyes. What could she do? Would accepting her gift help him? Not if he wouldn't see her. "I'll send my prayers."

"Yeah, he needs them."

"You hang in there, Bobby. Stand strong for all of them. If you need me for anything, please don't hesitate to call. He'll make it through this." Desperation tinged her words.

"Thanks. I'll talk to you soon, okay?"

"Okay." She hung up, then sat hugging herself, fighting back the tears.

Laughter sounded from around a corner. Maggie and Thomas strode into the yard, hand in hand, wrapped in a joy all their own. He stopped and pulled her to him, then he kissed her, burying his hand in her hair while she looped her arms around his neck and pressed her body close.

A lovers' kiss.

Erin shifted and they parted, glancing her way. Pink stained Maggie's cheeks, but her eyes were clearer than they'd been in a while. "Sorry, honey, you were so quiet, we didn't see you."

"So you two hooked up after all. When did this happen?"

Thomas took Maggie's hand, then led her to a chair beside Erin. He settled on Maggie's other side. "Remember that night we were all here and you and Tess brought out that wine and lowered the lights?"

"We were going to light the candles, too, but Maggie caught on to us and chased us out," Erin said.

"I asked her about that after you left. You see, I'd been thinking along those lines for the longest time, ever since your mom came back here to settle for a while."

Maggie squeezed his hand. "He means since I gave up men for a while."

"Right." Thomas smiled. "I'd been wanting to talk to her about the two of us, but we've been nothing more than friends for so long. I never knew how to broach the subject."

"Then you and your sister started with your nonsense and he wouldn't let up about it," Maggie finished for him.

Erin managed a smile. At last, a bit of happiness. "So you got together."

"Not right away," Thomas said. "I had to keep after her."

"I was worried about losing him as a friend."

"I told Tess that might be an issue." Erin picked up a piece of honey cake, then took a bite. Sweet. She'd forgotten how good they tasted.

"Well, I'm happy to say we worked it out." Thomas beamed. "I promised her my unending friendship no matter what happened between us, then I seduced her."

"Who seduced whom?" Maggie turned to Erin. "I seduced him."

"Anyway, I don't think either party needed much coaxing at that point." Thomas scooted his chair closer so he could wrap his arm around Maggie's shoulders. "The point is that I like that your sisters have settled for just one man."

Maggie beamed. "I told him I thought I might give that a try myself."

"That's great, guys. I'm so happy for you." Erin finished the cake, then brushed the crumbs from her fingers.

"So how are you?" Maggie asked. "Sophie says you haven't been yourself lately."

Erin told them all that had happened with Jack. "Bobby says he's given up. When I was last with him I got the feeling he blames himself because he survived and his sister didn't."

"That's horrible, honey." Maggie touched her hand. "You have to go to him."

"He won't see me."

"Ha." Thomas leaned forward. "I have never known that to stop a McClellan."

Erin stared at him. "You think I should see him, even though he doesn't want me there."

"He only thinks he doesn't want you. Once you get there, I'm sure you'll find a way to straighten out his thinking." Thomas gave her an encouraging nod.

"How?"

Maggie laughed. "It'll come to you. You're a McClellan, aren't you?"

Erin bit her lip. Was she truly a McClellan now? Could she embrace her gift? It all boiled down to Jack. He needed her. If embracing her gift was her best chance at helping him, then she was ready to do just that.

Confidence bloomed in her as she turned to face Maggie and Thomas. "Yes. I suppose am."

16

"ERIN." GRACE LANGSTON smiled broadly and stepped back from her front door. "Come in. Come in. It's so good to see you."

"Thank you." Erin stepped across the threshold into the entryway. She handed Jack's mother a basket of pasta and sauces. "I thought you might enjoy this."

"Thank you, dear. This wouldn't by chance be a bribe to get you in to see Jack?"

"Would it work if it was?"

"Then I'd say that you don't need a bribe. I'm thrilled that you've come. I would have called you on my own if you hadn't contacted Bobby. Can I get you anything—a soda, a glass of wine?"

"No, thank you. I didn't come here for you to entertain me."

"I suppose you didn't." A pained expression crossed Grace's face. "Bobby did tell you Jack isn't seeing visitors?"

"He told me Jack didn't want to see me in particular, if that's what you mean. But I intend to change his mind about that," Erin said.

"Well, I'm rooting for you. I wish there was more I could do. I'm afraid he's not going to be happy about this. At least, not at first."

Erin touched her arm. "It's okay. I accept full responsibility. How is he?"

"Physically he's doing okay, but emotionally… Dr. Carmichael is concerned that he's been slow to regain his strength. He has Jack doing physical therapy. Unfortunately there isn't a way to repair the damaged part of his heart. Being sick has really shaken him. I've never seen him like this before. He's always been the one we all looked to for everything."

She pressed her hands together. "I can see now that I was wrong to depend on him so much. I think before the attack he was trying to show me that in the gentlest of manners, but I didn't catch on until too late."

"I'm sure it's okay. Jack never wanted to let you down." Erin glanced beyond Grace into the interior of the house. "Where is he?"

"He's on the porch. At least he's getting fresh air. I'll show you." She led Erin through a cozy living room to a set of French doors. "Erin, since you're here, would you mind if Rose and I did some shopping? We're almost out of some of the basics and it would give the two of you some privacy."

"Please go right ahead."

"Thank you, dear." Grace squeezed her arm. "And good luck."

After she'd gone, Erin squared her shoulders and pushed through the doors. Wind chimes stirred in a slight breeze. Jack sat in a chair that rivaled Aunt Sophie's favorite lounger. A plaid blanket covered him.

He turned toward her. Surprise flickered in his gaze. He'd lost weight and strain etched his face. He lifted his chin and kept his expression neutral.

She shook her head. Silly man. Should she tell him she could feel everything he felt? His relief at seeing her reached out and touched her along with his deep joy, but overshadowing them both were the same feelings of guilt and despair she'd sensed in him in the hospital. He held on to his emotions, subdued them, but they were as clear to her as the November sky. He cared for her, and that was all she needed to know.

"Hi." She moved toward him, telling him with her eyes how glad she was to see him.

He glanced away. "I'm not really up to company."

"So I hear." She set her purse on a glass-topped table, then helped herself to a spot beside him on the lounger, smiling inwardly when he scooted over the smallest fraction to make room for her. At this point she'd take anything.

She straightened the blanket. "So how are you?"

The muscles in his jaw bunched. "I've been better, if you really want to know."

She covered his knee with her hand. "That's why I'm here. Talk to me."

"You wouldn't understand."

"Try me."

He stared out into the yard. "Stacey was a gymnast. Competed on a national level. She was a star athlete. She used to come here with her girlfriends and they'd spend the whole day doing their flips and whatever you call them." He pointed to the edge of an overgrown garden area. "There used to be railroad ties there. They used them like makeshift balance beams."

He paused and pain rolled off him, until Erin's throat tightened and her eyes burned. "One day she fell and she never got up."

"Jack…"

"What kind of world is this where a sixteen-year-old with her whole life ahead of her dies like that?"

"You feel guilty that she died and you didn't."

He didn't answer, but the sorrow in his eyes spoke for him.

"It was part of her soul's journey to die young." She touched his cheek and longing poured from him at the contact. "It wasn't part of yours."

He placed his hand over hers and the connection hummed between them. "I feel so lost, baby."

"Let me help you. You are a good man. You love your family. You're willing to die for them. No one could ask any more than that. You can't keep beating yourself up over this."

"For the longest time I tried to be there for them. I thought if I could do everything my dad and Stacey would have done, I could help make up for their loss. This illness has made me realize how impossible that is."

"Your family loves you for who you are, not for what you do for them," she said.

"I realize that. They've bent over backward for me these past weeks. Believe me, that's been a little hard to take."

He looked away. She took his face in her hands. "You have every reason to be here, to be taken care of. You have the rest of your life ahead of you and I want to be there with you. Please come back to me. I love you, Jack."

Longing filled his eyes and for a moment he struggled with the demons of his past, then he spoke her name in a whisper rough with emotion. She kissed him, her lips caressing his, coaxing him to let go of his fears and walk with her into the future. Their future.

With a sound of surrender he swept her into his

arms and gave in to the kiss, his tongue tenderly stroking hers while his hands smoothed over her back, then delved into her hair.

She held on and kissed him with all the love in her heart. When his hand covered her breast, she pulled back, frowning. "I believe you need a doctor's clearance to do that."

He closed his eyes. When he opened them, desire shone in their depths. "But touching you, feeling your skin against mine, joining my body with yours is the strongest medicine. I want you, Erin. I have wanted you since the first time I saw you."

"But your heart."

"Love me, Erin." He opened the blanket to her. As he gathered her close, she sighed.

"I can't refuse you when you look at me like that."

"I'll wrap this over us both. They can't see us here from inside."

She smiled as she moved beneath the cover with him. "They've all gone. We're alone. But we're taking this slow and we're stopping at the first sign of trouble."

"Slow and easy." His mouth covered hers and he kissed her as if they had all the time in the world, his tongue dancing slowly with hers.

This time when his hand cupped her breast she reached back and unhooked her bra, then guided him up under her shirt. His fingers worked their magic on her, beading her nipple to a hard point.

Breaking the kiss, he moved to nuzzle her ear while she slipped her hands up under his pullover. She caressed his chest, circling outward until her fingers found the scar from his surgery. He helped her yank his shirt over his head, then she pressed her lips over the ridge of raised tissue and rolled his nipple between her thumb and forefinger until he stilled her hand.

She pulled back to look at him. "Are you okay? Do we need to stop?"

"I don't want to stop. I need to see you." He pulled her shirt off and dropped it on top of his, then her bra followed. "Straddle me."

She did as he asked, and he hooked his fingers in her waistband and pulled her forward, urging her up-ward, bringing her breasts to the level of his mouth. She gasped as his lips closed over her and his tongue circled her nipple.

"Oh, Jack, that feels so good, but this is supposed to be about you."

"But this is about me. This is about what I want, and right now this is what I want." He took her again into his mouth and suckled her until she moaned and pressed against him.

His hands gripped her bottom. He caressed her, slipping his fingers between her legs to rub her through her jeans. Then he tugged at her waistband and her pants loosened. Her zipper rasped.

"These have got to go." He pulled the offending garment off first one leg, then the next, until she straddled him wearing just her panties.

He ran his hand over her hips, appreciation shining in his eyes. Then he pulled her close again and kissed her, slipping his hands down to cup her bottom. She opened his pants, then freed his erection, holding him with a firm grip.

She kissed his ear. "I want to kiss you here." She ran her hand up the silky length of him. "Would that be all right?"

"I think I can suffer it."

His soft moans floated over her as she loved him with her mouth. She explored every sensitive inch of him with her lips and her tongue before she took him into her mouth. He withstood several moments of her slow, steady loving before he gritted his teeth. "Sweet woman, stop and let me come inside you."

She left him to retrieve her purse. "Allow me," she said as she rolled a condom in place.

Smiling, she moved back up him, teasing him by rubbing her breasts against him as she removed her panties. Then she guided his wondrous cock inside her. She took him with slow, steady strokes, riding him at a leisurely pace, each stroke of her body drawn out for maximum enjoyment as she caressed him with her inner muscles and brought the sensual tension coiling around them.

Holding his gaze, she let him see all the pleasure he brought her, not holding back a single moan or sigh. "It feels so good to have you inside me, Jack. I want to do this to you every day you're able until you're all better and then I want to love you some more."

"Oh, baby, you've got the magic. I love what you do to me." He held her hips and guided her as his breathing became shallow and his moans increased.

She loved him gently, tenderly, and he gave her back the same, whispering endearments as he held her close. She came a beat ahead of him, both crying out, then collapsing together under the soft blanket.

His heart thrummed steadily beneath her palm. Her gaze met his and warmth cocooned them. She snuggled close and kissed him, then drew back, her own heart brimming. "I love you, Jack."

He nodded, half smiling as sleep claimed him. She lay beside him for long moments, stroking his chest and listening to the beat of his heart. Then she rose, careful not to disturb him. After tucking the blanket securely around him, she dressed, then kissed his forehead.

As she headed back to her car she stifled the little bit of disappointment that surfaced in her. So she'd told him twice that she loved him and he hadn't once returned the sentiment. It didn't matter.

He loved her. She'd felt it in every fiber of her being as he'd made love to her. She'd seen it in the way he'd looked at her.

He loved her and one day he would say the words. For now she was satisfied in more ways than one. She'd come with a goal. Come hell or high water she'd meant to break through to him. She glanced back at the house as she pulled away and smiled.

Mission accomplished.

JACK CAME SLOWLY AWAKE, wrapped in a dream that was too good to be true. Erin had come to him. She had touched him and she had loved him and she had spoken those magical words.

I love you, Jack.

He sat up and pulled the blanket tighter around him. She had said the words and he hadn't said them back. The first time he'd been overwhelmed by the power of her words, too caught up in the emotion to form any word beyond her name. Then she'd said them again, it seemed, as he'd drifted to sleep, and he'd dreamed of her, dreamed of finding her and telling her he loved her, too.

He rose, shivering. Dusk had fallen and the temperature had dropped. He grabbed his shirt, then hurried to shower, energy filling him as it hadn't…well, since the last time they'd made love.

He showered, then dressed, then whisked his cell phone from the nightstand. She answered almost immediately, her voice filled with warmth. "Jack. How are you?"

"Better, much better. Ready to conquer the world."

"I'm so glad to hear that." A myriad of voices sounded in the background.

"Where are you?" he asked.

"At my aunt's. We're having Nikki's bridal shower. Want to come?"

"Really?"

"Yeah, if you're up to it. I could come get you if you want."

He hesitated, still hating to ask for help. "I can probably get Bobby to drive me, though I feel like I could do anything at the moment."

"I want Bobby to drive you. If he can't, call me and I'll come get you."

"Okay." He grinned. "So you really want me to come to this bridal shower?"

"All the guys are here, too. Thomas, who we can't pry off Maggie—that's my mom—but the guy's been waiting decades, so who can blame him? Then Dylan and Mason are here. Even Sophie has a date, one of

Mason's uncles. If you come, I won't be the odd one out anymore."

He inhaled a deep breath. If asking for help meant he'd see Erin that much sooner, then it was well worth it. "Let me call my brother."

"Tell him he's welcome to stay and join the party," she said.

"I will. Oh, and Erin, there's something very important I have to tell you, but I want to tell you in person."

"Okay. Hurry. I'll text message you the address and directions."

Hurry he did. Bobby was thankfully available. For once Jack was able to ask for help and not feel guilty. Bobby seemed pleased to be of assistance. The traffic lights shone favorably on them and they pulled up to Erin's aunt's house less than thirty minutes later.

"This is it, Bobby. There's her car." Jack nodded to her car, lined up with a number of vehicles pulled to the curb in front of the house. Anticipation rolled through him.

Bobby shook his head as they headed up the porch stairs. "I can't get over the change in you. It's miraculous."

"Never underestimate the power of love—or in this case, the power of the McClellans, which I'm coming to believe is synonymous."

The front door swung open before they reached it and Erin threw herself into Jack's arms. She kissed him soundly, then pulled away, smiling. "Come in and meet my family."

"Wait." He tugged her hand. "This is the family you have nothing in common with? The one you don't like to talk about?"

"It took me a while to realize it, but I've finally accepted that we have more in common than I wanted to admit. Now come in. I want them to meet you."

"Wait." He tugged on her hand again. "I have that something to tell you and I want to tell you in private and I can't wait another minute."

"Oh, Jack, I love you."

"Damn it, quit saying that," he said.

"But I do. I love you."

"But that's what I want to tell you. Now you're making me look bad because you've said it so many times and I haven't."

"You two are nuts. Is it okay if I go in?" Bobby asked Erin.

"Please do and tell them I'm going to be a while. Jack seems to be having trouble telling me what he wants to tell me, but tell them I still love him anyway."

"Erin." Jack pulled her hard up against him, then he kissed her before she could say another word.

She melted into his arms and he decided he liked

kissing her probably as much as he was going to like telling her he loved her, so he kissed her longer, until she melted a little more and he was fairly certain she'd be at least out of breath.

Then he pulled back and looked deep into her sea-green eyes. "Erin McClellan, I love you. Now will you make an honest man of me? Because the more we're together, the more obvious it is that we can't keep our hands off each other. I think the best way to take care of that is to get married."

Her eyes rounded and her smile widened. "Married? Are you sure?"

"Absolutely. I want you to be my wife and make passionate love to me at every opportunity."

She cocked her head, her lips pursed. "What about the other? Were you okay today…you know… after?"

"Oh, actually I was great. I'd forgotten all about that. Must have gotten everything purged the last time."

"But what if it happens again?" she asked.

"I don't care. I love you and I want to be with you. Always. So what do you say? Will you marry me? I don't have a ring because I didn't know I was going to ask you until I did, but we can pick one out tomorrow."

"Don't you want to meet my family first? I mean, before you commit yourself to a lifetime with them?"

"Nope. I already know I'll love them."

She nodded and her eyes darkened. "Then yes, Jack. I will marry you."

He pulled her close and kissed her, then kissed her again for good measure, just because he could. "So I guess it's time to meet everyone."

"We don't have to. We could sneak away to my place and make love some more," she said, her voice hopeful.

"Let's do that later."

"Okay, but you should know they really are a little out of the ordinary."

"But you've come to accept that, haven't you? Even though you're this normal kind of girl."

"Well, about that normal thing. I have a confession to make," she said.

"Yes?" He smiled as he took her hand and they headed for the door.

"I was faking it."

HARLEQUIN®

Blaze™

COMING NEXT MONTH

#219 GIVE ME FEVER Karen Anders
Red Letter Nights

When Tally Addison's brother goes missing, she knows who to turn to—gorgeous ex-cop Christian Castille. Only, when she and Christian stumble into a search for hidden treasure, she discovers she's already found hers...in him.

#220 HOT SPOT Debbi Rawlins
Do Not Disturb

She's got the sexiest man in America and Madison Tate is going to...take his photograph? In fact, she's counting on the hot picture to win a magazine cover contest that could make her career. But when Jack Logan balks at even removing his shirt, Madison knows she'll have to use a little feminine *persuasion*.... Good thing the photo shoot is at the seductive Hush hotel....

#221 ALL I WANT... Isabel Sharpe
The Wrong Bed

Krista Marlow wanted two things for Christmas—a sexy man and a lasting relationship. Well, she got the sexy man one night when she and Seth Wellington ended up in bed in the same cozy cabin. But would the relationship survive New Year's once Seth revealed his true identity?

#222 DON'T OPEN TILL CHRISTMAS Leslie Kelly

Social worker Noelle Bradenton has never believed in Santa. But when a thieving St. Nick drops cop Mark Santori at her door, Noelle has to rethink her opinion of Christmas. Because Mark is one present she'd definitely like to unwrap....

#223 GETTING IT NOW! Rhonda Nelson
Chicks in Charge

TV chef Carrie Robbins would do anything to get her show off the ground—even parade around half-dressed! But when the network hooks her up with stuffy British chef Phillip Mallory, she's ready to quit...until it becomes obvious that the oven isn't the only thing heating up....

#224 FASCINATION Samantha Hunter
The HotWires, Bk. 1

Sage Matthews's fascination with computer hacking got her into deep trouble. Just ask FBI agent Ian Chandler, who arrested the fiery redhead—and has been watching her every sexy move since. Now she's ready for a fresh start, but Ian's fascination with her is about to bring him more trouble than he ever imagined.

www.eHarlequin.com

HBCNM1105